HEMLINES, HANDBAGS & HAVOC

A Dogwood Springs Cozy Mystery

SALLY BAYLESS

Paperback ISBN: 978-1-946034-34-2

Kimberlin Belle Publishing LLC

Contact: admin@kimberlinbelle.com

Publisher's Note: This is a work of fiction. Names, characters, places, and incidents are a product of the author's imagination. Locales and public names are sometimes used for atmospheric purposes. Any resemblance to actual people, living or dead, or to businesses, companies, events, institutions, or locales is completely coincidental.

Cover art by DLR Cover Designs, www.dlrcoverdesigns.com.

Chapter One

"IS everything okay with the historic fashion show, Libby?" My best friend, Cleo Anderson, pushed back the bangs of her blond pixie cut and looked at me. "You seem stressed."

"I am facing some challenges." This Saturday, August 10, the local history museum of Dogwood Springs, Missouri, where I served as director, was hosting an event in the high school auditorium.

I stood and angled the umbrella over our table at the Dogwood Café. We'd just sat down for Sunday dinner, and the August sun, still hot even late in the day, had been hitting both of us at a bad angle.

"What's going on?" Cleo asked.

Bella, my golden retriever, nudged my thigh with her nose.

"Hold on," I told her. I sat back down, dug into my big purse, and brought out a doggy treat.

She happily took it, lay down in a protected corner near

our table, and began chomping so loudly that I heard her over the hum of conversation from nearby tables.

I looked back at Cleo. "Although ticket sales have been strong, I'm desperate to find a seamstress to repair some of the dresses and I'm struggling to line up amateur models. I thought everything was set, but I lost two models yesterday. One woman came down with a horrible case of poison ivy, and the other fell and broke her ankle."

"Oh, wow." Cleo shook her head. "What a bummer."

Cleo and I shared a house where she rented the upstairs apartment and I rented the downstairs. We were close in age, with her being thirty-one and me thirty-three, and when I'd moved to town more than a year ago, we'd become fast friends.

Would she be willing to help me out?

She was always working on craft projects, and she loved fashion. Plus, she was bubbly, energetic, and bold. I knew she'd be comfortable on stage.

I raised an eyebrow at her. "Any chance you want to take on some sewing projects or reconsider being a model?"

Cleo shook her head. "I wish I could be in the show, but my parents and I are visiting an elderly cousin in Jefferson City that day. It's her birthday. And as much as I love craft projects, I'm not very good at sewing actual garments."

I nodded, disappointed but not surprised. It had been a long shot.

"I would think lots of women would be happy to be models." Cleo pushed her oversized glasses higher on the bridge of her nose.

I shook my head. "That's what I thought. Just like I thought it would be easy to find a seamstress to do the repair work we need. Wrong on both counts."

For styles from the past century, we'd feature models wearing vintage garments. But dresses made prior to 1920 were often fragile and too small to fit modern women. A friend of mine was the curator at a museum in Indiana, and for the earlier styles, they'd loaned us period-correct re-creations.

Unfortunately, those loaner outfits had come with the warning that some of them weren't in the best condition, and my curator friend hadn't exaggerated. We really needed a skilled seamstress.

Earlier in the summer, I'd been excited about hosting the fashion show. I loved historic garments, and I'd hoped the show would be a fun way to draw more visitors and support for the museum. And normally, when I ran special events, I had everything well-organized. This time, though, I was flailing. Every time I got something figured out, another aspect of the event fell apart. We'd had to switch locations and dates, and last week we'd lost our emcee, which left me filling in.

Plus, we were supposed to have ten models, but now we'd lost two. And two of the dresses on loan were in such poor shape that they couldn't be worn. In the best-case scenario, with eight usable dresses and eight models, it would work out. But not every dress fit every woman, which meant I only had six women with dresses they could model.

A server came to our table, and Cleo and I placed our dinner order. He returned almost immediately with my iced tea and her Diet Dr. Pepper.

She unwrapped her straw and slid it into her glass. "So, what are you going to do about the fashion show?"

I let out a long sigh. "I don't know. I hate to cancel. Maybe I should postpone it." I didn't like that idea either, though. I'd already switched the date once and then heavily promoted it.

Cleo looked toward the entrance of the fenced-in outdoor seating area, then grinned at me. "Hey! The solution to one of your problems just walked in. See the woman in her fifties in the light blue dress? The one with mousy brown hair desperately calling for highlights?"

"I do." Cleo—who ran the most popular hair salon in town—tended to think half the population needed highlights, but her instincts were usually right. She'd cut my brunette hair so it brushed my shoulders and moved when I turned my head. Then she'd added subtle highlights that perfectly complemented my green eyes and made my skin appear less pale.

Cleo waved at the woman she'd indicated. "That's Bobbi Sue Ellis. She's one of the best seamstresses in town. She's who my mom uses."

"I've heard she's wonderful, but she hasn't returned my calls. I've left three messages." Maybe, since she knew Cleo's family, I might be able to convince her to help me.

Cleo halfway stood and waved again at the woman. "Hey, Bobbi Sue."

The woman's face lit up, and she made her way over to our table.

"Hi, Cleo," the woman said. "Nice to see you."

"Bobbi Sue, I'd like to introduce my friend Libby Ballard. She's the director of the Dogwood Springs History Museum, and I think she could use your help."

I stood to greet her, and I introduced Bella.

"What a beautiful dog." Bobbi Sue patted Bella's head and scratched behind her ears.

Bella loved her immediately.

"My name may be familiar," I said. "I'm the person who called about the historic dresses and the fashion show."

"Historic dresses?" Bobbi Sue's eyebrows scrunched together. "I'm sorry. I've been out of town with my sister, and I left my assistant in charge of the shop. She's wonderful with a needle and thread and with people who stop in, but she probably never even checked the messages."

"Oh." Maybe I had a chance. "Please, join us." I gestured to an empty chair.

"Just for a moment." Bobbi Sue sat down. "I'm picking up a carryout order. Tell me more about these dresses."

"The museum is putting on a historic fashion show this Saturday. For styles before 1920, we borrowed some authentic re-creations. But some of those dresses need repairs that are beyond my skill level."

"I've got a little time in my schedule. How many dresses are we talking about?" Bobbi Sue asked.

Hope bubbled through me. "There are two dresses that need repair. Plus, there's one more with a ripped hem. I could do that one," I volunteered. I wasn't a great seamstress, but I could fix a hem.

Bobbi Sue leaned in. "What about the others?"

"The first one is a rose-colored re-creation of an 1876 princess-line style that needs work on the bodice. I think someone must have worn it who needed a larger dress. The side seams are about to fall apart."

"Excuse me, ladies." Cleo stood up. "My salon is closed because the air conditioner is on the fritz. We've been able to contact all the clients to reschedule except one, and she just walked in." Cleo hurried across the seating area and followed a blond woman inside the café.

Bobbi Sue and I resumed our conversation, discussing the needed repairs. She gave the impression she could work them in. The only question was, could the museum afford her services?

"So now comes the hard part." I shifted slightly in my chair. "What do you think all that might cost?"

"I do love the idea of your event," Bobbi Sue said. "My sister and I are both crazy about historic fashion. We even drove to Washington, DC, two summers ago to see the exhibit of First Ladies' dresses at the Smithsonian Institute."

"I love that exhibit," I said quickly. Our eyes met, and I knew I'd found a kindred spirit.

"I know it's kind of last minute." Bobbi Sue paused. "And you probably have everything lined up. But is there a chance you need two more models?"

My pulse quickened. Seriously? Could this conversation get any better? "You and your sister?"

She nodded eagerly.

I studied Bobbi Sue, thinking of the dresses we had available. She was the perfect size for one of them, but the other dress would only fit someone much smaller. "Does she wear about the same dress size as you do?"

"Hardly," Bobbi Sue rolled her eyes. "Patti's a tiny thing. Barely a size 6."

Yes! "This is incredible. I was just telling Cleo that I recently lost two models. I think you and your sister might be perfect."

Bobbi Sue's eyes lit up, and she clapped her hands together like an excited child. "Really? We can both be in the show?"

"You'd need to try on the dresses. They're two of the actual historic garments, so I'd hesitate to alter them. But I think they will fit."

"That would be such a thrill for us. If you're offering that—and I know you can't control if the dresses fit—I'll do all your repairs, including that hem, which will take me a fraction of the time it would take you, for free."

For free? I forced myself not to jump up and down and cheer. I shouldn't take advantage. This woman was a professional seamstress. "I couldn't ask you to do that."

"I'd be delighted," she replied.

"Are you sure?"

"I'm positive." She glanced toward the door to the café. "I'd better go. I bet my carryout order is ready. Shall Patti and I come by the museum tomorrow to try things on and pick up the dresses you want altered?"

We arranged a time in the afternoon, and she headed inside to get her dinner.

I sat back in my chair, gazed out at Main Street, and let out a slow, relieved sigh. Then I leaned down and patted Bella on the head. "Isn't that amazing, Bella? Both of my problems solved simply by coming here."

Bella looked up at me, her eyes gleaming as if to say that I should have never worried.

"And wasn't Bobbi Sue's response exactly what I should have expected from someone in Dogwood Springs? People here are so kind." Yes, I'd had a bit of bad luck setting up the fashion show, but now things were running smoothly.

"Whew." Cleo appeared beside me and sat back down. "That client sure can talk. How did things go with Bobbi Sue?"

I grinned. "Fantastic. Not only is she willing to do all the repairs for free, but I now have two new models. My problems are solved."

"Excellent!" The server approached with our meals, and Cleo leaned back to let him set down her bacon cheeseburger.

"I know. I can hardly believe it." I beamed as the server placed a pork tenderloin sandwich and the café's famous coleslaw in front of me.

Finally, after all my problems, everything was going to work out perfectly for the fashion show. I turned to Cleo. "So, what happened to the air conditioner at the salon?"

Chapter Two

THE NEXT MORNING, I awoke to the sound of doggy toenails click-click-clicking across the hardwood floor of my bedroom. A moment later, a furry someone was breathing near my pillow.

"Bella, it's not time yet." I opened one eye at the clock, glanced over at her, and slowly sat up. The alarm was going to go off in ten more minutes anyway, and her warm brown eyes gleamed with love as if there was nothing she wanted more in the world than to spend time with me.

Once again, I was reminded of how foolish I'd been when I'd adopted her, thinking I was doing her a favor by taking her in. In reality, I'd been the lucky one. She'd changed my life by giving me so much love and joy.

I got out of bed, rubbed her ears while I told her good morning, and let her out into the backyard.

While she was outside, I thought about how easily my

worries over the fashion show had been resolved when Cleo and I had eaten dinner at the café. Wouldn't my staff be thrilled when I told them the news?

Before long, Bella and I had eaten breakfast and were ready for our regular morning walk down Elm Street to Thirteenth Street, where we would turn around and come back.

"Come on, Bella." I grabbed her leash and snapped it on, then opened the front door.

The white, two-story house Cleo and I shared had been built in 1900. Even when new, it hadn't been anything fancy, and modernizations over the past century had been economical, not high end. Still, it had a bit of history, and I'd choose it any day over a brand-new, cookie-cutter apartment.

At just after eight, Elm Street was waking up. One of my retired neighbors was setting up a sprinkler where he'd replanted grass, car doors slammed, and engines roared to life as many of my younger neighbors headed off to work. Luckily, I didn't need to be at the museum until nine, which allowed Bella and me to get our walk in early. By the time we turned around to head home, humidity already hung in the air.

Along the way, Bella greeted each person we met—a mom out with her baby in a stroller, a teenage boy who ran by in a cross-country T-shirt, and a pair of retired brothers excitedly discussing the recent winning streak of the St. Louis Cardinals—with her tail wagging and head high, ready to share some golden-retriever love. Bella had belonged to the previous renter of my apartment before he'd passed away. After I adopted her, I'd quickly realized three things: she was well-behaved, incredibly smart, and already friends with everyone on the block.

Everyone except the squirrels, that is. But this morning, the squirrel population was lying low, and we arrived back home without any loud barking incidents.

I showered and got dressed for the museum in a black skirt, an emerald-green silky blouse, and black flats. As a final touch, I added my favorite accessory: the pearls that had belonged to my great-great-grandmother. Although I'd only moved to town about a year ago, she had once been the mayor of Dogwood Springs.

While Bella was outside soaking up a few more moments of sunshine, I made sure she had plenty of clean water, filled her favorite toy with peanut butter, and hid it behind a chair in the living room. Then I called her inside, hugged her, and told her how much I loved her. Finally, I grabbed my lunch and big black purse and headed off to start the day.

The museum was only a fifteen-minute walk away, a stroll that took me through most of downtown. Leafy green maples shaded Main Street, and cute shops and restaurants with colorful awnings lined both sides of the street. Huge baskets filled with pink, purple, and white petunias hung from each light post, and pots of annuals added more color by the doorways.

Several shop owners were out and about, whistling as they watered the flowers and swept the sidewalks. Add in the beautiful green hills around the town and the sweet scents drifting out of the bakery and the candy shop, and Dogwood Springs was a pleasure for all the senses. With an award-winning winery nearby—and thanks to the tourist trade, a far greater number of fine restaurants than most towns its size—no wonder the place was so popular.

And if, after all the idyllic scenery, anyone had doubts about whether it was a nice place to live, then the kindness and caring of the residents as well as the fact that the town had both an independently owned bookstore and a large, well-stocked library settled the question.

Soon I reached the Dogwood Springs History Museum on the far side of downtown. The two-story white Greek revival, built in 1920, had originally been the home of local businessman Charles Pennington. He'd generously left a trust in his estate that allowed a little town like Dogwood Springs to have a history museum with a full-time director and a staff of two.

Of course, as it was for the director of any nonprofit organization, fundraising was a key part of my job. Currently, though, between the trust fund, fees from local visitors and tourists, and donations from other generous individuals, we weren't in bad shape. Since I'd become director a little over a year ago, we'd installed a new HVAC system, and we'd put in an elevator that allowed all visitors to access the second floor. That also made it much easier for my staff and me to install displays.

The museum wouldn't open to the public until ten, so I

walked around back to the door that once had led to the kitchen and now opened into our conference room.

My two staff members, Rodney Grant and Imani Jones, had already arrived and were sitting at the long conference table, discussing the merits of the flavors of the three doughnuts Rodney had brought.

"Libby?" Rodney waved a hand at the small bakery box. "What's your pleasure?"

Rodney, a quiet man in his sixties who served as the museum curator, had a full head of gray hair, a ruddy complexion, and a delightfully dry sense of humor. Today, as he did most days in the summer, he wore a store-brand polo shirt and khaki pants.

The aroma of Rodney's favorite dark-roast brew filled the air, but I bypassed the coffee and popped a mug of water in the microwave to brew some tea. "Is that one in the corner a sour cream cake doughnut?"

"It is indeed," Rodney said.

"I think that one's got my name on it."

Rodney had probably planned the chocolate for Imani and the blueberry for himself. I set my donut on a napkin, added a bag of some strong black Yorkshire tea to my cup, and put it on the table next to where Imani was sitting.

Imani, the museum's education coordinator, was about five years younger than me and had a growing collection of vintage '60s clothes. She was tall and slender and often wore her box braids pulled back into a low bun. Today she had on a blue-and-purple geometric print dress that hit above her knees and a pair of strappy sandals. She was a lot of fun, and even though she had a nine-month-old at home, she had a seemingly boundless supply of energy.

She tapped the edge of the donut box. "I was surprised at first that Rodney didn't bring in our usual muffins from the bakery downtown, but this new donut shop is surprisingly good." She grinned and took a big bite of the chocolate-frosted donut.

"Take a look, Libby." Rodney gestured to a chair across the room where an antique parasol sat folded up.

I carefully rinsed my fingers, dried them, and examined the repairs he'd done. "This is great. Such a fine example. Right about 1900?"

Rodney nodded. "Yes, it's one of the donations we received from that lumber baron's family."

"I've got to be sure to include this in the fashion show and explain how some women used them for self-defense at the time." I set the parasol back on the chair and removed the tea bag from my mug.

"I love stories about that topic," Imani said. "There were even classes that taught umbrella self-defense techniques. It will be great information for the show. You know, disputing the notion that fashion was all lace and ribbons."

"Exactly. And speaking of the show, I've got big news." I sat down and shared the story of my conversation with Bobbi Sue Ellis. "I can't tell you how glad I was when she offered to do the alterations and repairs for free. I was getting afraid we might have to cancel or postpone the event." I took a bite of my donut, savoring the fluffy texture and the rich, sweet flavor.

Imani wiped some chocolate frosting off her face and glanced over at Rodney. "Uh, Libby, are you sure you want Patti Sue Harrison to take part in the historic fashion show?"

I did a double-take. "The sisters' names are Bobbi Sue and Patti Sue? Isn't that a bit much?"

Neither Rodney nor Imani replied. They just stared at me as if waiting for me to answer Imani's question.

My shoulders tightened. "Why wouldn't I want Patti Sue in the fashion show?"

"Because she is, without a doubt, the most difficult woman in town," Rodney said.

"Really?" I looked from him to Imani. "Is she that bad?"

"Well ..." Imani shrugged one slim shoulder. "My momma has a saying about those two. 'Bobbi Sue,'" Imani's voice softened as she imitated her mother, "'is a mild-mannered cutie. Patti Sue is a pain in the patootie.'"

Hmmm. I'd never met Imani's mother, but from what Imani had said about her, I imagined she didn't speak unkindly about many people, much less come up with a rhyme about them. I sat back in my chair, my stomach churning.

"Knock, knock?" a voice called as the back door cracked open. Alice VanMeter, president of the museum's board of trustees and our number one volunteer, as well as a dear friend of mine, poked her head inside. "Do you all mind if we interrupt your Monday muffin time?"

I'd forgotten Alice had planned to bring by a new friend

she'd told me about. And apparently, our routine of starting the week with baked goods was no secret.

Rodney, Imani, and I intentionally only bought three treats each Monday so we wouldn't overindulge. We didn't have more to share, so we quickly polished off our donuts.

"Come on in," I called out.

Alice, a woman in her mid-fifties, walked into the kitchen, followed by a tall woman with short chestnut hair who appeared to be of a similar age.

"Hi, everyone." Alice gestured to the other woman, who was wearing hyacinth-blue cotton pants and a coordinating blouse. "This is my new friend, Valerie. I've been telling her about the museum, and she's decided to become a volunteer. I brought her in early so I could show her things in the gift shop before we opened."

"Nice to meet you, Valerie." I introduced myself, as well as Rodney and Imani.

Valerie quietly said hello. When she smiled, lines crinkled around her mouth and eyes as if—despite what Alice had told me about her—in happier times, she had spent a lot of time smiling.

Valerie and her husband had lived in California until a year ago, when their entire town was destroyed by a forest fire. For a while, the community tried to rebuild, but after about three months, everyone gave up.

Although they died before she was born and she had never visited the town as a child, Valerie's maternal grandparents had once lived in Dogwood Springs. Because of that, she and her husband had come here on vacation about ten years ago.

When their California town could not recover from the fire, they decided to move here. Unfortunately, less than a month after they arrived, Valerie's husband dropped dead from a heart attack. They had no children and no other surviving family, and Valerie was left very much alone. Alone, that is, until she met Alice. Having been befriended by Alice when I moved to Dogwood Springs to build a new life, I knew how fortunate Valerie was to have met her. Steady and nurturing, Alice would support Valerie as she adjusted to the deep losses she had suffered.

Rodney cleared his throat. "Alice, what's your experience with Patti Sue Harrison been like?"

Alice's forehead furrowed, and she gave a slow shake of her head.

Beside her, Valerie visibly stiffened.

"You've met her too, Valerie?" Imani said.

"No, but my husband and I were warned about her when we were hunting for an apartment. I was surprised because everyone else we met was so kind."

Rodney and Imani both turned to look at me.

Uh-oh. I may have gotten myself into a mess. "Fine, I'll admit it. I never should have agreed that she could be a model in the fashion show before I talked to you guys, but I can't refuse now. It would be horribly rude. Besides, the museum and its events are for everyone in the community, not just the people we like."

Alice dipped her head in acknowledgment, but no one said a word.

We'd planned a simple historic fashion show—an hour and a half long including a short intermission. The models would walk out, I'd stand by the microphone, describe their clothing, and give some historical context. They'd walk off the stage, and everyone would go home happy.

"She's only one woman," I said. "Even if she's difficult, how bad can it be?"

Chapter Three

OVER THE COURSE of the week, Patti Sue fully lived up to her reputation of being a pain, what with her disparaging comments about how the other models looked in their dresses—which I immediately contradicted—and her queen-bee attitude. Despite her, things began to fall into place. Bobbi Sue's sewing work was flawless. And the models learned how to walk on stage to best display the dresses.

On the day of the fashion show, the Dogwood Springs High School auditorium was packed almost to capacity. The crowd, which was mostly women, buzzed with conversation that drowned out the period music we had playing.

I slipped out the door where Alice was working the ticket desk, hurried down the auditorium hall, and turned left into the main hallway, my flats clicking against the gray tile floor. There, on my left, between the boys' and girls' bathrooms, was a door to a stairwell that led backstage. On my right, amid a wall of blue metal lockers, was the door to the classroom we were using as a dressing room.

I knocked on the door and checked on the models inside. Fern, Diane, Edna, Noreen, Melissa, Julie, and Jade wore dresses representing styles from the 1860s up to the 1920s. Two of the models of more recent styles were already backstage, but Patti Sue, who was wearing a lemon-yellow suit from the 1940s, had accidentally popped out a contact lens and dashed to the girls' bathroom. When I called into the bathroom, she assured me she would be in position on time.

My phone alarm buzzed in my back pocket, alerting me that I needed to get into position myself. I silenced the alarm and slipped up the stairwell to backstage. Bobbi Sue and Valerie, wearing dresses from the 1950s and 1960s, were waiting in the wings right of the stage, ready to go on.

I gave them a reassuring two thumbs up, walked through the crossover space behind the curtain, and smiled at Rodney, who was sitting in the left wing ready to work the curtain.

A tingle ran down my arms. All the planning and hard work were coming together. With luck, this would be the first of many historic fashion shows, an annual event the museum could count on to entice more visitors to the museum, draw in more volunteers, and convince towns-people to donate to the nonprofit's coffers.

I skimmed the notes on my phone one last time, then nodded to Rodney and signaled to Imani, who was working the control board in the back of the auditorium. She flick-ered the house lights, and Rodney opened the curtain.

The room fell silent.

This was it! Showtime!

I walked to the left front of the stage, blinked at the bright lights, and lifted the mic from its stand. Then I drew in a deep breath and began. "Welcome to the first annual historic fashion show, put on by the—"

"We can't hear you," someone called out loudly.

Drat. We'd checked all the tech an hour ago, and it had been working fine. I shot a panicked look at Imani, who held up one finger, did something with the control board, and motioned for me to go ahead.

"Put on by the—" My chest tightened. The mic still wasn't working. Was there another one I could use? Or would I have to try to talk loudly enough for everyone in the room to hear me?

That was probably impossible, given the whir of the air conditioner.

I looked back toward the soundboard, but Imani wasn't there. Where—?

Oh, there she was, hurrying down the aisle, making some indecipherable gesture with her hands.

I shook my head.

Imani dashed up on stage. "Jiggle the mic cord," she whispered.

"What?"

"Jiggle the mic cord."

I did as she instructed and tried again. "Hello?"

My voice filled the room, and the crowd cheered.

"More than ten years since I graduated, and the high school still hasn't replaced these mics," Imani muttered. "Just jiggle it again if it gives out."

"Thank you," I mouthed, and I turned back to the crowd.

"Let's try that again," I said into the mic, and I stood taller. "Welcome to the first annual historic fashion show put on by the Dogwood Springs History Museum. I'm delighted to see all of you here today." As I'd practiced, I gave them a wide smile.

"We'll be going back in time today, working our way from the 1960s back more than one hundred years to the mid-1800s when Dogwood Springs, then called Silersville, was founded. We've got some amazing garments to show you, and I'll be offering some commentary on the period of each outfit to give you more context. Before we begin, though, some thanks are in order."

I scanned the crowd, hoping the high school principal had been able to join us, but I didn't see her. "First off, thanks to the Dogwood Springs High School for letting us use their auditorium. Although we're fortunate to have lovely display space at the museum, including a new display area on the second floor, we can't seat three hundred." I paused and reminded myself to slow down.

"In addition, I want to offer a big thanks to my staff members, Rodney Grant and Imani Jones, to the museum's many wonderful volunteers, to all of you who support the museum financially, and to our models for the day." I glanced across the stage at Valerie, who was in the wings, smoothing the skirt of her dress. "And now, without further ado, let's begin."

I looked out toward Imani, but she had already started the folk-rock song we'd chosen to create the atmosphere for the 1960s.

"Our first dress, modeled by Valerie Johnson, is a fine representation of styles from the late 1960s."

The spotlight hit Valerie as she came onstage. She was missing the long, narrow, orange scarf that should have been draped around her neck, but otherwise, her ensemble was fine, and she walked confidently, pausing at the mark on the stage as we'd discussed.

"I have to say a special thank you to Valerie," I added. "A newcomer to Dogwood Springs, she's not only recently become a volunteer at the history museum, but she was also willing to model in our show today."

Valerie's cheeks grew pink, and I returned to the script. "When you think of the early 1960s, the style icon was First Lady Jacqueline Kennedy. I'm sure you can picture her wearing a boxy skirt suit with a pillbox hat, white gloves, and a short triple strand of pearls."

I stopped, allowing Valerie time to turn at the front center of the stage.

"The dress Valerie is wearing has a much different vibe, a vibe from the late sixties when the cultural focus shifted to youth, when designer Mary Quant of London brought us the mini-skirt, and when crowds of teenage girls were caught up in Beatlemania. At this point in fashion history, hemlines took a bolder jump up, with dresses stopping at mid-thigh."

I'd been so grateful that Valerie had been willing to wear the minidress. She had the height the dress needed, and some of the other amateur models had said that there was no way they'd wear a dress that short. Valerie, though, had been willing, as long as she could wear pantyhose to hide the fact that her legs were, in her words, pasty white and slightly dimpled.

I'd quickly agreed that wearing pantyhose was fine.

I continued the script I'd memorized. "This sheath dress, created in a bold avocado and orange print, is from 1967. Note the relaxed feel of this dress and the matching unstructured purse. Also in that period, you might have seen a similar dress in silver polyester, worn with white patent leather boots, a nod to the nation's focus on astronauts at the time, which culminated in the moon launch the entire country watched with fascination on television on July 16, 1969.

"Normally, Valerie wears her hair differently, but today she's styled it more like the classic pixie cut of the times. For an icon from this period, think of the British model Twiggy." I added a bit more context, mentioning the political issues of the 1960s, as well as key societal and cultural issues. Where I could, I explained how those elements were reflected in the fashion of the day.

"Thank you, Valerie," I concluded.

Exactly as we'd rehearsed, Valerie made one more slow spin and exited stage left.

Not bad. Minus the orange silk scarf, but not bad at all.

"Now let's slip almost fifteen years back in time. Bobbi Sue Ellis has been invaluable to our show. She's not only one of our models, but she's also lent her sewing expertise to repair some of our dresses. She's wearing an outfit characteristic of the early 1950s."

Right on cue, the music shifted to an early rock and roll classic.

Bobbi Sue walked out onto the stage, eyes widening, steps slowing. I'd warned each of the models that the lights would be bright and the crowd large, but maybe I should have emphasized it more.

I gave her my most encouraging smile.

She returned a not-very-convincing smile of her own.

"While not as formal as you would picture his designs, the hourglass silhouette here echoes that of Christian Dior's New Look, which he introduced in 1947."

At the mention of Dior's name, a murmur of appreciation ran through the crowd, and Bobbi Sue's shoulders suddenly relaxed. She walked to the front of the stage and slowly turned, exactly as we'd practiced.

The crowd watched, appearing entranced.

My own shoulders eased in relief. Despite the tech issues and nervous models, we just might pull this off.

I refocused my mind on my script. "We see the classic nipped-in waist and full skirt, here in a wild pink floral skirt supported by petticoats of nylon mesh ..."

I paused while Bobbi Sue lifted the skirt slightly to show the petticoat, then continued. "The skirt is paired with a plain, snug-fitting pink twinset. This emphasis on the decorated skirt may be familiar to some of you in the classic poodle skirt that is often associated with 1950s fashion."

A few audience members nodded.

"The adjective I'd use to describe this era of fashion would be elegance. Women reveled in the freedom following World War II when greater availability of fabrics and greater wealth allowed for a bit of extravagance. Note the cat's-eye glasses, matching accessories, and Bobbi Sue's bouffant hairdo. When you think of getting ready for the day in the early 1950s, think of teasing your hair, using lots of hairspray, and wriggling your way into a girdle to create that nipped-in waist."

I continued into political and social issues of the day, letting everyone get a good long look at the skirt and sweater set, then thanked Bobbi Sue, who slowly walked offstage.

I silently cheered. As jittery as she'd seemed when she began, I'd been afraid she'd dash out of the limelight as fast as possible. Instead, she'd blossomed.

Next up, Patti Sue.

"Our next garment," I said, "is a gorgeous lemon-yellow suit from the 1940s." The music changed to a big band hit, just as we'd planned. "The padded shoulders and rounded collar are classic for the period."

I stopped and stared hopefully at the far side of the stage, then stifled a groan.

No one could see those padded shoulders because Patti Sue had missed her cue.

I cleared my throat and spoke louder. "This suit, worn by Patti Sue Harrison, once belonged to the aunt of another of our models, Noreen Dawson, and was purchased at an upscale department store in Chicago called Marshall Field & Company."

Still no Patti Sue.

"Um, pardon me a moment, ladies and gentlemen. We seem to be having another technical issue." I returned the mic to the stand and scurried into the wings to the right of the stage, where Patti Sue should have been waiting, ready to go on.

But no one was there.

I dashed behind the curtain to the left wings, where Rodney sat, ready to close the curtain after the first act, and where Bobbi Sue and Valerie had stayed after exiting the stage. "Where's Patti Sue?" I hissed.

Rodney glanced around. "No idea."

"Earlier, she was in the girls' bathroom with Jade," Bobbi Sue said.

"They were arguing," Valerie said. "I heard them when I ran back to get my purse. Something about candy bars ...?"

I blew out a frustrated breath and turned to Valerie. "Can you go get her?"

"Will do." Valerie darted toward the backstage passageway that opened near our dressing room.

Scrambling to think how I could stall, I stepped back onto the stage and picked up the mic again.

If only I'd listened when people told me what a pain Patti Sue would be. Not only had she made snippy comments about the other models every time we practiced, but she'd gotten involved in some argument backstage—one I had no doubt she'd started—and missed her cue.

What was taking so long? Should I skip to the next model, Jade? I caught Bobbi Sue's eye and mouthed for her to run and tell Jade to be ready to go on, then turned back to the audience. "I'm so sorry about that. I'm afraid we'll have to wait a few more minutes to see 1940s fashion. Let's skip to the 1920s. I'll set the stage for you by telling you a few of the key historical and cultural elements of the day."

People in the audience began murmuring and shifting in their seats.

Aargh. Listening to a history lesson was not nearly as interesting as seeing dresses with information about the time period sandwiched in between. This was exactly why I'd gone into museum work, not become a history teacher. I wanted history to be accessible—and inviting—to everyone. Tangible items could make history come alive.

Except when a certain mean-spirited busybody missed her cue ...

I told myself to focus.

"When you think of fashion of the 1920s," I said, "almost everyone's mind goes to the flapper-style dress."

Imani adjusted smoothly, starting up an instrumental jazz piece. I paused, trying to recall the next line of the script.

And a high-pitched scream pierced the air.

～

The crowd went completely silent. Then a young girl, who was sitting with her mother in the front row, began to cry. Conversation erupted, and several people stood and began to move toward the aisles.

What on earth? I looked back toward Imani, and then at Rodney. Off to my left, Alice peeked her head in the door from where she'd been manning the ticket desk in the auditorium hall.

Officer Tate, a member of the local police department I'd met on more than one occasion since I moved to Dogwood Springs, suddenly stood in the audience. "Everyone, please remain seated and keep calm," he said in a loud voice. "I'll see what's going on."

Imani turned up the house lights, and I beckoned Alice up the stairs to the side of the stage and angled my head toward the audience. "I'm going with Officer Tate. Tell them about the opportunities to volunteer at the museum as well as how someone can become an annual or a lifetime member. Oh, and if the mic cuts out, jiggle the cord."

"Will do."

I handed the mic to Alice and fell in step behind the officer as he stepped into the wings.

Officer Tate paused and told Rodney to stay put but—perhaps because it was my event—allowed me to go with him. We skirted a jumbled pile of lighting equipment and crossed behind the curtain, all the while searching to see who might have screamed.

Once he'd checked backstage, we made our way down

the staircase and through the narrow passageway to the main hall.

There, off to our left, the models stood in a tight cluster. Jade silently pointed at the floor near them, but a large cleaning cart blocked our view.

We walked around it, and I froze. For a second I couldn't catch my breath.

Patti Sue Harrison lay crumpled on the tile floor.

Valerie knelt on the other side of Patti Sue, her avocado floral sheath washed out in the hallway's fluorescent lights. Her face had gone as pale as milk.

In contrast, Patti Sue's face was dark red, a hideous sight against her lemon-yellow suit and bright 1940s red lipstick.

An orange silk scarf was looped around her neck, and a mark ran across her throat right above it.

Chapter Four

"STEP AWAY FROM THE BODY, MA'AM." Officer Tate's voice echoed in the hallway, and his tone left no room for argument.

"She's ... she's dead." Valerie's eyes were glazed, and her hands shook as she slowly stood and backed toward me. "I held my hand under her nose, and there was no breath, and I ... I ..."

I started to put a hand on her arm, but Officer Tate told me to stop.

"We'll need to check her clothing for trace evidence," he said.

"Oh." I hadn't thought of that. Things seemed to be happening too fast. One minute I was on stage, starting the fashion show. The next minute I was here, at the scene of a murder.

A few steps away, Bobbi Sue let out a sob, and I realized

that Jade was holding her back, perhaps to keep her from seeing the body too closely.

I glanced down at Patti Sue's body and my chest tightened.

Her white gloves were crisp against the yellow of her suit, but the seams of her stockings were crooked. And her chignon, previously so carefully pinned up, had partially come undone as if she'd struggled before she died.

Yes, Patti Sue had been, as Imani said, a pain in the patootie, but no matter how mean-spirited she was, she hadn't deserved this. She hadn't been all bad. Despite the difficulties she'd created during rehearsals, she had truly been excited to be in the fashion show, even willing to squeeze her feet into peep-toe pumps that were a size too small because they went with the outfit.

The question was, who could have killed her?

The scarf that looked like it had been used to strangle her was clearly the one that went with Valerie's dress. And Valerie hadn't been wearing it when she came onstage.

But she looked too horrified to have killed Patti Sue.

I pressed my lips together. Some event organizer I was. I'd been angry with Patti Sue for missing her cue, thinking she was having an argument with someone in the restroom, and the whole time she'd probably been lying here dead.

Maybe that argument—I shot a quick glance over at Jade—or another disagreement she'd had was what led to her death.

Beside me, Valerie shuffled her feet and wrapped her

arms around herself as if she was trying to hold herself together.

"You're going to be okay, Valerie," I said. "The police needing to check your clothes for evidence is only a precaution. You might have removed a hair or something else from the killer when you checked on Patti Sue."

Valerie nodded silently, but her eyes remained wary.

Officer Tate spoke into his phone while he checked the body. "I'm almost certain she's gone," he said, "but send the EMTs just in case."

He stepped back and turned, blinking as if momentarily confused by all the different dress styles.

I had to admit, it was an odd-looking collection of people to have at a crime scene. Valerie in her avocado 1960s sheath. Bobbi Sue in the pink floral skirt and twinset of the 1950s. Fern in a turquoise 1860s-style gown with its enormously wide skirt. Melissa looking like she'd just stepped out of 1895 in a gown with huge, puffy sleeves. Julie in a re-creation of a walking suit from 1915, which hit right above her ankles. Diane in an 1872-style dress with a large bustle. Edna in a rose-colored re-creation of an 1876 princess-line gown. Jade in a purple flapper dress. And Noreen in a blue dress in the style of an 1890s Gibson Girl.

A disconnected selfish sorrow washed over me at the sight of all those gorgeous garments that our audience wouldn't get to see. The clothes from later in the 20th century were fascinating, of course. But it was the dresses representing styles from farther in the past that would have stolen the show, which was why I'd planned the program going back in time, saving the best for last.

Officer Tate called me over to stand with him on the other side of the hall, his eyes narrowed. "Libby, how many entrances to the school are open?"

"Just the one at the end of the hall to the auditorium. The door at the end of this main hall is locked, and they've got those metal barricades up." I pointed. "All that's accessible is the auditorium hallway and this part of the main hallway with the bathroom and these four classrooms."

"That's all?"

"There are fire doors in the auditorium that lead outside," I said. "But they only open from the inside and they set off an alarm."

"And I guess everyone had access to the crime scene." He peered down the hall. "Because it was near the restrooms."

"Yes, but I saw Patti Sue alive no more than five or six minutes before the show started because I came back here to check on the models. And Alice was sitting at the ticket desk, so if someone came this way after that, she should remember. The show was almost ready to start, so most people would have been in their seats."

"Good," Officer Tate said. "That helps."

I heard a siren, distant at first, but growing closer.

His phone rang. He answered and backed away with his eyes on Valerie and the crime scene the entire time.

A minute later, he hung up and walked back toward me. "They'll be keeping everyone in the auditorium. Eventually, we can send most of those people home as long as we get their names. If you'd like, we can share those names with you so you can provide refunds."

"Refunds ..." My heart sank. I'd been so focused on the fact that people wouldn't get to see the gorgeous dresses that I'd forgotten about the more practical goals of the event—raising money and attracting visitors and donors to the museum. None of which was probably going to happen.

I was still digesting that thought when two EMTs and two uniformed officers I didn't know rounded the corner from the hall to the auditorium, followed by Detective John Harper.

"Libby." The detective nodded to me, stepped aside to let the EMTs pass, and went over to talk to Officer Tate.

After a brief conversation, Officer Tate and the two uniformed officers headed toward the auditorium. Detective Harper walked toward the rest of us. His mouth was pressed into a thin line, and his eyebrows, which were much darker than his salt-and-pepper buzz cut, were drawn together.

He asked the models several questions. I didn't intentionally eavesdrop, but the show was my event and I couldn't help but be curious.

Eventually, the detective stepped closer to me. "Are you doing okay, Libby?"

"Yeah."

"Tate told me what you said. Is there anything else you can tell me?"

"No. I don't have a clue who did this. But I'm sure if I

ask a few questions, I can figure out a reason why Patti Sue was killed."

"Hold on, there. I simply wanted information. I'm not in any way encouraging you to try to find the killer."

"But—"

His body stiffened. "You are not a member of law enforcement. Even if you've been lucky in the past solving crimes without getting killed, you need to stay out of this. Everybody's luck runs out eventually."

We'd had this conversation before. He thought I was nosy and stubborn. I knew that I was good at solving puzzles, even good at figuring out who had committed a murder. I was observant and logical, and—because I'd been treated unfairly in the past—justice mattered to me. When I ran into unfairness, dishonesty, or injustice, it really bugged me.

I shot another glance at Patti Sue's body.

Oh, I knew, intellectually, that her death wasn't my fault. If someone wanted to kill her, they could have done it anywhere. But based on who had access, it seemed like the culprit might be someone involved in the fashion show.

There was a very real chance that if it hadn't been for the show I'd planned, Patti Sue might not have been murdered.

That evening, after the police finished questioning witnesses and we were allowed to go home, I sat in my living room with Bella at my side, her head resting on my knee. I pulled a cozy afghan around my shoulders, more for comfort than for warmth, and ran a hand over the soft fur on my dog's head. "Oh, Bella, today was a disaster."

She snuggled her body closer to my leg as if she sensed my pain and wanted to make me feel better.

I bent down to hug her, soaking up her love and calm presence, and a knock sounded on my back door.

I walked into the kitchen, and Cleo was peering in through the door, waving at me. I opened the door, and Bella wriggled out, eager to greet her.

"Libby, I'm so sorry. I told my parents we had to leave Jefferson City as soon as I got your text." Her words tumbled out, and she dropped her purse on the same corner of the counter as mine and then hugged me. "I can't believe someone was killed at your fashion show."

"I can't believe it either." I motioned for her to follow me into the living room. "I mean, I know Patti Sue wasn't exactly popular, but it was awful."

I sat back down on the couch, and Cleo took the tan armchair across from me.

Bella walked over to Cleo, thumped her tail against the upholstery of the chair, and flopped down on the floor between us.

"Do the police know who the killer was?" Cleo leaned forward.

"I don't think so. I mean, I think they were able to rule out most of the audience because they were all seated, waiting for the program to start. There wasn't that long of a window of opportunity between when I talked to Patti Sue and when her body was discovered. But there were several people who had access to the area where she was killed, that main hallway where the bathrooms are and the back-stage door lets out." I looked over at Cleo.

She nodded. A graduate of Dogwood Springs High, she must have walked through that hallway hundreds of times. Sometimes, as a person who'd only moved to town about a year ago, I forgot how well most of my friends knew the area.

"Did Patti Sue have problems with anyone in the show?" Cleo asked.

"Yes, but—"

"Wait." Cleo threw up a hand. "Let me guess. Detective Harper told you not to get involved."

"In no uncertain terms." I shivered, remembering his warning. *You are not a member of law enforcement. Even if you've been lucky in the past solving crimes without getting killed, you need to stay out of this. Everybody's luck runs out eventually.*

Rather hard to forget.

My phone dinged with a text.

Sam Collins
Something happy to get your mind off
Patti Sue's death—my mom just called.
She and my dad are coming to town
Saturday and want to go to dinner with us.
They can't wait to meet you.

I sank lower in my chair.

Cleo leaned in. "What's wrong?"

I held out my phone so she could read the text.

Her forehead crinkled. "That's good, isn't it?"

"Sam's been saying they were going to come visit for a while now. I know I need to meet them, but how am I going to convince them that I love Sam for who he is, not for his money?"

"Oh." Cleo bit her lower lip. "I guess when you date someone as rich as Sam, that is an issue."

Sam Collins, the man I've been seeing for about a year, was a really special guy. Smart, funny, and kind. He'd also made a fortune in tech back when he lived in California. "I've been dreading this for weeks and—"

My phone rang. "It's Alice," I said. "I'd better take it." I answered the call.

"Libby," Alice sounded stressed.

"Is there news about the murder?"

"Detective Harper considers Valerie his prime suspect," Alice said. "He says the murder weapon was part of her outfit and that she was seen in the hallway where Patti Sue was murdered about the time it happened."

Emotions swirled inside me. Disbelief that the detective had focused on Valerie when she seemed so shocked by finding the body. And a lingering hint of guilt that perhaps if I hadn't hosted the fashion show, Patti Sue might still be alive.

"Cleo's here," I said. "I've been telling her what happened. Can I put you on speaker?"

Alice readily agreed and, after Cleo could hear the conversation, repeated what she'd told me about Valerie.

"The poor woman's a mess, and who can blame her?" Alice said. "She lost her home, she lost her husband, and just when she was starting to make friends and build a new life here, the police suspect her of murder. It's too much."

I pulled in a deep breath then released it slowly. "Oh, I feel terrible, Alice. I'm the one who sent her to find Patti Sue when she missed her cue. Does the detective seriously think Valerie strangled Patti Sue and then came on stage and modeled just as we'd practiced?"

"It's crazy. All because the murder weapon was her scarf," Alice agreed. "She had it earlier, but when she rushed backstage after getting her purse, she realized she'd lost it. She said the scarf wasn't mentioned in the script, so she figured she'd be okay. And she didn't have time to hunt for it."

That did make sense. "So, it may have fallen off when she was hurrying to get her purse—"

"And the real killer picked it up and used it," Cleo said.

"That's what I think," Alice said. "I don't know why Detective Harper can't figure that out. Sometimes he latches onto the first suspect and never goes any further." She let out an audible sigh. "Libby, are you going to try to find the real killer?"

I sat for a moment, thinking about Valerie and all she'd gone through, thinking about the fact that, as far as I knew, she didn't have any motive for killing Patti Sue, and thinking about how this latest tragedy would reflect on the museum. Even if I only got involved for professional reasons, this murder needed to be solved.

Detective Harper's warning echoed again in the back of my mind.

I didn't want to be stupid, didn't want to end up dead.

But if the man couldn't figure out who the murderer was, someone needed to. The real murderer needed to be behind bars. Valerie needed to be able to build a life here in Dogwood Springs. And the museum needed to move past this.

"If I did try to find the killer"—I looked over at Cleo—"would you both help me?"

"You bet," Cleo said.

Alice's voice rang through the phone. "Absolutely. And you know the rest of our friends would help too."

I sat up taller. "Alice, can you ask Valerie if she can meet with you, Cleo, Zeke, Sam, and me tomorrow afternoon at the Dogwood Café?"

"Why don't we meet at my house?" Alice suggested. "I think Valerie might be more comfortable without people at other tables staring at her and whispering. About two o'clock?"

I glanced at Cleo to see if that time worked for her. She nodded.

"That sounds smart, and two is fine with us," I said and ended the call. So like Alice, always thinking of other people's feelings.

I squared my shoulders and turned to Cleo. "I'll text Sam to accept the invitation to dinner, and I'll worry about his parents later. It looks like we've got a new mystery to investigate."

Chapter Five

BY THE TIME Cleo and I left for Alice's on Sunday, Alice had decided that because it was a rare cooler day, we'd all be comfortable at her patio table under the umbrella, and she invited Bella to come along.

"Did you see Alice's text?" Cleo asked as she, Bella, and I walked out to my car. "She's making banana cake with cream cheese frosting."

"I did. I can't wait to taste it." Alice was such an excellent cook that I knew it would be delicious.

Bella seemed disappointed when I offered her a seat in the back instead of her favorite spot, riding shotgun, but she climbed in and leaned her head forward between the seats.

A few minutes later, we drove into an upscale neighborhood and pulled up in front of Alice's two-story brick house. Bella eagerly scrambled out of the car.

Alice waved from the front step and led us through to her kitchen, which opened onto a lovely patio.

Valerie was already there. She gave us a quick wave, but her smile didn't match the lines around her eyes or the way she clutched her arms over her midsection. This poor woman. After all she'd been through, now she was suspected of a horrendous crime.

Bella hurried over to say hello.

"I hope you're okay with dogs." I should have asked Alice to check.

Valerie pulled out a chair from the patio table, sat, and immediately began petting Bella. "I love dogs." Her voice rang with emotion. "What's this sweetie's name?"

I introduced Bella and Cleo, and, while Bella and Valerie got better acquainted, Cleo and I helped Alice bring out the bowls, spoons, and napkins, as well as a pitcher of iced tea and one of lemonade. Perhaps I was projecting, but it felt as if Valerie was grateful Bella was there, as if she might feel more comfortable with a dog than new people. Probably how I would feel if the police considered me a top murder suspect.

"Hello." Sam appeared from around the corner of the house carrying a reusable grocery bag.

My heart did a little flip-flop, and Bella left Valerie to trot over to him.

As always, Sam looked incredibly handsome. His dark hair was slightly messy in that way that seemed like he'd just run his hands through it. He had on tan shorts and a navy St. Louis Cardinals shirt that showed off his biceps. Add in his dark, rectangular-framed glasses and he was the very definition of a sexy geek.

But as good-looking as he was, it was his personality that drew me to him. He had a great sense of humor and was kind, easy-going, and curious. I could see why he'd been so successful in business. He was fascinated by new ideas and comfortable with risk.

"Sorry Bella abandoned you, Valerie," I said. "This is Sam Collins. It didn't take long after he and I started seeing each other for Bella to decide he was one of her favorite people."

"I have that effect on everyone." Sam laughed. "Seriously, nice to meet you, Valerie." He shook her hand. "I know you're new to town, and I'm sorry the police are making that transition more difficult."

"Nice to meet you too." Lines eased around Valerie's eyes. "Until this happened, it seemed like such a lovely town. So restful and pretty. Hopefully, I can get past this and be able to appreciate it again."

"I bet you will." Sam held up his grocery bag. "I should ask Alice for a scoop for this."

"Oh?" Valerie looked at the bag. "What did you bring?"

"Minnesota's Pride ice cream." Sam pulled out a carton of peanut butter with chocolate swirls.

Cleo and I chuckled. "He's sort of addicted," I explained to Valerie.

"That flavor should go great with the cake I saw on the counter." Zeke, Cleo's sixteen-year-old nephew, walked out of the kitchen. Tall and lanky, he had a long, dark ponytail and wore a black T-shirt and tan shorts, along with black flip-flops. "Sorry I'm late. I was over at Zoe's."

Over the past few months, Zoe Thompson, a girl a year younger than Zeke but in the same grade, had gone from being "a friend" to a pretty serious girlfriend. The two of them seemed made for each other—both smart, level-headed, and fascinated by computers.

I introduced Zeke to Valerie. I imagine, to her, he may have seemed like an odd addition to our group since he was just getting ready to start his junior year in high school. But his sharp mind, tech skills, and contacts at the high school had proved invaluable when our group had solved mysteries in the past. And, like the rest of us, he was inquisitive and enjoyed figuring things out.

After he met Valerie, Zeke knelt down to say hello to Bella.

"No Doug?" Cleo asked Alice as she brought out the cake.

"No." She let out a sigh. "He's in North Carolina, talking with a candle company about including their products in his gift baskets."

The way she mentioned her husband's business so casually, a newcomer like Valerie might not realize that Doug's online gift-basket company was hugely successful. Which was most likely the way Alice wanted it. She was never one to brag.

I sat by Sam, and the rest of the group joined us at Alice's round picnic table. Bella settled down near Valerie, almost as if—in her special Bella way—she sensed that Valerie needed a little extra comfort.

Just seeing my friends made me more confident that we

could figure out who the murderer was. Each of these people was as dear to me as family, and I knew they would do their best to help Valerie.

"Hey," Cleo said. "Before we discuss the murder, I have news. My parents agreed to co-sign a loan with me, and I've put in a bid to buy the building my salon is in. Everybody, cross your fingers for me."

"Wow." My roommate was buying commercial property downtown. "Good luck."

Everyone murmured their encouragement.

After a moment, Sam looked across the table at Alice. "What about you? You're also taking a big step. Are you ready to start fall classes?"

"I am." She began slicing the cake and passing around bowls and the ice cream carton. "I was registered for two classes, and I added another. It's not a full load, but it's all I can manage while scaling back some of my volunteer duties around town. And thanks for the tour of campus. I appreciate the study spots you showed me."

Alice turned to Valerie. "After Sam sold his big tech company in California, he became a member of the computer science faculty at Grove University."

Valerie nodded. Despite the casual chit-chat that might have made her feel more at ease, she still seemed uncomfortable.

"Let's dive right into discussing the murder," I suggested.

I poured myself a glass of iced tea, and an ice cube split

in two with a loud crackle. "Valerie, tell us about when you found Patti Sue in the hallway."

Valerie pressed her lips into a narrow line and then described things almost exactly as Alice had told me. She had been ready to go on stage, realized she didn't have the green floral purse that matched her dress, dashed back to find it, and in the process, lost her scarf. And when Patti Sue missed her cue and I sent Valerie back to find her, Patti Sue had already been dead.

It sounded completely reasonable to me, and I struggled to see how she would have had time to strangle someone. Plus, I remembered how shocked and pale she had been in the hallway by the body.

"Did you and Patti Sue have any arguments?" I asked.

Valerie shook her head. "No. I heard her make a few catty remarks to some of the women in the show, but she never seemed to target me."

I winced. Not only had I put on an event where someone had been murdered, but I'd brought in someone who targeted the other participants with mean comments. There was nothing I could do about those comments now, and Patti Sue had more than paid the price for them.

All I could do was act kindly and fairly with the information I had, and that meant trying to find the person who had killed Patti Sue. Which my gut told me was someone other than Valerie.

I glanced at the others and sensed that they agreed with me.

"Let's consider the other suspects," I said.

Valerie let out a sigh.

I took a quick sip of my tea. "Thirteen people were involved in the fashion show—me, Imani, Rodney, and ten models. But only three people besides Valerie had access to the main hallway at the time of the murder: Jade, Noreen, and Edna. I had sent Bobbi Sue from backstage to get Jade, but she arrived in the hallway after Valerie found the body. And the other models were in the dressing room together the whole time."

"Could a woman have committed this crime?" Alice said. "I mean, would they have had the strength?"

"I looked it up, wondering the same thing." And wondering if Detective Harper had zeroed in on Valerie because she was tall and appeared quite fit. "It doesn't take that much strength. The victim is defenseless because the killer approaches them from behind. And Patti Sue was petite and fine-boned, built rather like a little bird."

"The meanest bird I ever saw," Cleo muttered.

"Garroting someone is generally thought of as a man's crime," Zeke said. "But if a woman was sneaky, using that means of murder might confuse the police."

"You're right," I agreed. "The timing of the murder and the use of the scarf may have been opportunistic, especially if it was a crime of passion. But the killer may have planned the murder, using that specific method of killing, and been waiting for the right time."

"Can you explain where everyone was?" Sam said.

"Sure." I pictured it in my head. "Bobbi Sue was in the wings with Rodney. Imani was in the back of the auditorium running the sound and light board. Alice was in the auditorium hall at the ticket desk."

"Not that we suspect you, Alice," Cleo said.

Alice smiled, and I continued. "Fern, Diane, Melissa, Julie, Noreen, Jade, and Edna were all in the classroom we were using as a dressing room. From what I overheard them tell Detective Harper, Fern, Diane, Melissa, and Julie were together the whole time. The other three—Noreen, Jade, and Edna—each stepped out at one point to go check their dresses in the full-length mirror in the girls' bathroom. We don't know exactly when the murder took place. Just that it was sometime between when I talked to Patti Sue a few minutes before the show started and when Valerie found the body."

Zeke scratched the back of his head. "I can understand that the body was hidden by the cleaning cart, but even if they had the classroom door closed, wouldn't they have heard someone strangling Patti Sue in the hallway? And gone out to check?"

Cleo leaned in. "Sue Ann, the dispatcher for the police, came in earlier today to get her acrylic nails done, and I asked her that very question. She explained that since Patti Sue was so petite, she may not have been able to put up much of a fight." Cleo shuddered. "And, of course, she wouldn't have been able to cry out."

Alice tapped a fingernail on the table. "There's something else to consider. We only had one door open from the auditorium to the auditorium hall, and I was sitting beside it. To get to the murder scene, someone would have needed to go past me and turn left around the corner into the main hall. Two people from the audience did that before the show."

"Who?" Cleo asked.

"Trent Miles and Chip Wasserman, who were both at the show with their wives. Trent said he was going to use the restroom and would be right back, and Chip walked by on his phone as if he needed privacy for a call."

"I know Chip," Sam said. "But let's go through each of these people so I can get them straight in my mind."

"Good idea," I agreed. "Let's start with Chip. Sam, how do you know him?"

"He's on faculty at Grove University. He's a pretty big deal in the biology department. Has a large research lab."

"Can you think of a reason he'd want to kill Patti Sue?" Cleo asked.

"No. I can't even imagine how their paths would have crossed," Sam said. "He's not the kind of person to get involved in community volunteer work or anything. It is a small town, though, and I guess Patti Sue annoyed a lot of people."

Alice and Cleo exchanged glances.

"You can say that again," Cleo muttered.

"What about Trent?" I asked. "I don't know him."

Alice waved a hand. "I do. He runs a greenhouse that's next door to Hartley Road Apartments, the complex Patti Sue owns. He always seemed like a pleasant person to me, and I don't know of a reason he'd want to kill her, but he probably knew her."

"Don't people normally go to the nursery in Westfield?" I asked. If anyone would be familiar with greenhouses in the area, it was Alice. The woman loved plants.

"They do for big stuff," she replied. "But if you need a bag of fertilizer or a few annuals to fill a pot, Green Thumb Gardens is right here in town and reasonably priced."

"So those are the only people besides the participants in the fashion show who had access to the murder scene?" Zeke asked.

"As far as I know," Alice said.

"Let's talk about the fashion show models, then." I held up a thumb, ready to count them off. "First—"

"Libby, I hate to interrupt," Valerie said. "But what about the water heater guy?"

I turned to her. "What water heater guy?"

"White hair, my age or thereabouts. He had on a gray T-shirt and blue overalls with a little red faucet embroidered on them. He was in that utility room by the girls' bathroom muttering about the water heater and some kind of buildup."

Alice's eyebrows rose. "That's Gene Harrison. He's a local plumber."

"And he's Patti Sue's brother-in-law," Cleo added.

"I bet someone from the school let him in before we even arrived," Alice said.

Wow. I'd had no idea he was there. "I did notice that there was no hot water in the girls' bathroom."

"I noticed that too," Alice said. "Which means Gene had a legitimate reason to be in the hallway. He always seems like such an easy-going guy. I can't imagine him killing someone."

"We definitely need to include him as a suspect, though." I added him to my mental list. "Let's go through the fashion show models. Who knows Noreen well?"

Alice waved her hand again. "I do. From my volunteer work at the hospital. She's in her thirties and works as a nurse in the ER."

"Which would mean she would know where to apply pressure to strangle someone," Sam said.

"On the other hand," Valerie said quietly, "most nurses I've met have been very caring people. And I got to know Noreen a bit at the fashion show rehearsals. She never mentioned any issues with anyone in the show."

"Okay," I said. "We're keeping her on the list, though. At this point, we're including everyone who had access. What about Edna Hughes? I know she's retired, and I think she used to work in a local insurance agency." I glanced over at Cleo and Alice to see if I was right.

They both nodded.

"She's very quiet," I continued. "But she seemed comfortable on stage in practice."

"She's sung solos in the community choir, which gave her stage experience," Alice said. "And she lives next door to Patti Sue, but I've never heard Edna say anything against her."

"They could have had a dispute over a property line," Zeke said.

"Good point," Sam agreed.

"I know Jade," Cleo said. "I do her hair. She told me that before she started coming to me, she had a terrible time. Not every salon in rural Missouri is up on the current styles for Black women. She's in her early twenties and works for Patti Sue as the office manager at Hartley Road Apartments."

Sam sat down his glass of lemonade. "I have known workplace tension to get pretty ugly."

"We also know Jade argued with Patti Sue, right before the fashion show started," I said. "I don't know what it was about though. Someone mentioned something about candy bars …?"

"Actually"—Valerie scraped a spoon across her bowl, getting a dollop of cream cheese frosting—"I overheard some of that argument. I didn't want to discuss it in front of Bobbi Sue because it made Patti Sue look so bad. Patti Sue told Jade that if she didn't eat so many little candy bars at work, the dress she was modeling would fit better. She went on and on about it and was downright vicious."

I held back a sigh. If only I could go back in time and not make the decision to include Bobbi Sue and Patti Sue in the fashion show. It would have turned out a lot better for Patti Sue, of course, but also for everyone else involved.

"Typical Patti Sue," Cleo said. "What did Jade say in response? Or was she too afraid to say anything?"

"She came right back at her. Said she had loved working for Patti Sue's husband before he died and Patti Sue took over running the apartments, but that Patti Sue was so mean that …"

"That what?" Zeke asked.

Valerie winced. "That she wished Patti Sue was dead."

"Wow." Cleo spread a hand over her chest. "Did you tell Detective Harper?"

Valerie shifted in her chair. "I did, but he said it sounded like I was trying to push the blame off on someone else." She studied her bowl. "Which is probably how it sounds to you as well."

"That's not how we approach things," Alice said.

"Nope." I met Valerie's eyes. "We talk to everyone just like we're talking to you, and we logically follow the clues. And I think the first person we need to talk with is Jade. Cleo, you know her, and your shop is closed on Mondays. Are you free to go with me to Hartley Road Apartments tomorrow at lunch?"

Cleo, who had just taken a bite of cake, gave me a thumbs up.

"Great. With luck, we can find someone Detective Harper should consider as a suspect besides Valerie. Tomorrow, we start by talking with Jade."

Chapter Six

LATE THE NEXT MORNING, after giving a tour to a group of tourists, one of whom tended to talk over me whenever I spoke, I escaped to my office to eat lunch at my antique mahogany desk.

When the museum building had been erected in 1920, my office had been a child's bedroom in the Pennington home. For a second I thought about how, if that child could have been suddenly transported to the present day, they would be amazed by my computer and my microwaved enchiladas. The internet, Mexican food, even the little plastic tray that held my enchiladas, all would have been unknown to a child in rural Missouri in 1920. About the only things that would have seemed familiar were the short-bread cookies I'd packed for dessert.

I pulled my mind back from my time-travel musings and ate my lunch, deleting emails from my inbox.

A minute before twelve, a text dinged on my phone.

Cleo had fed Bella, let her out for a few minutes, and was now in the museum parking lot, ready to pick me up.

I grabbed my purse, dashed down the back stairs, and climbed into her Jeep. "So where are we headed? I don't remember Hartley Road Apartments from when I was trying to find a place."

"It's not far past the hospital." Cleo turned back onto Main and followed it to where it intersected Hartley Road. "The units are about twenty years old, so you may have ruled them out if you wanted something historic."

I nodded because I probably had.

"Plus, they're not the area you wanted." Cleo stopped to let some tourists jaywalk in front of us. "But for people who work at the hospital, it's a convenient location. They used to be very popular. I haven't been there in a while, but I heard they've gone downhill."

Bryce Parker, a local veterinarian, stepped out of the Dogwood Café carrying a large takeout bag. He spotted Cleo and waved.

Cleo brightened and started to wave back, then quickly stopped herself and refocused on the road.

Odd. Back in high school, Cleo and Bryce had dated until she'd broken up with him. She'd come to regret that breakup, and, after living in New York, had moved back to Dogwood Springs a few years ago. She had hoped to win him back, only to learn he'd recently become engaged to someone else.

After his fiancée had been killed three months ago, she'd reached out to him to be supportive, and I'd thought they might start dating again. These days, though, Cleo never mentioned him.

I gave Bryce a quick wave, and the minute the tourists were across the street, Cleo drove on.

Should I ask her what had happened?

No. If she didn't want to talk about it, I shouldn't push. "Any word from your real estate agent about the salon?"

"Not yet. The wait is killing me." A few minutes later, Cleo turned into a complex of about twenty buildings, each two stories tall with two apartments on each floor.

Cleo was right. At one time, they had probably been some of the most upscale rentals in town. Today, they showed signs of wear.

She parked near a one-story building with a sign marked "Office" that listed Patti Sue Harrison as the owner and manager, and we went inside.

Jade was alone behind a desk with a nameplate that said she was the assistant manager. She was on the phone, running through info about the complex with a potential renter. She gave us a sweet smile, gestured to two chairs across from her desk, and then to a bowl of mini-candy bars.

Cleo and I each helped ourselves to a piece. After all, it would be rude to reject chocolate. While we waited, enjoying our treats, I scanned the room. Although it was spotless and the furniture was attractively arranged, the furniture and carpet seemed slightly worn just like the exterior of the complex. Not so worn that most people would replace them in a private home, but enough so that they didn't seem to fit an office that was selling apartment space.

"Whew!" Jade hung up, tugged the hem of her polo shirt down, and sat up taller. "Sorry to keep you gals waiting. I don't think that guy had ever rented an apartment before. I had to make sure he really understood all the bills he'd be responsible for."

A kind thing to do, at least in my opinion. "How are you doing after the tragedy this weekend, Jade?"

"I'm okay." Her voice sounded shaky. "Still a bit in shock, I guess. I've never known anyone who was murdered before." She glanced away for a second then looked at us. "Things are kind of up in the air here, of course, since Patti Sue owned the complex. For now, the accountant who handles the payroll says I've got a job, and I should just keep coming into the office and doing the same old thing." She hesitated. "And, I have to admit, selfishly, I was pretty sad that I didn't get to model that purple flapper dress. It's such a pretty thing."

"Yeah," I agreed. "It was a shame that the show got canceled. I'd love to try it again, but who knows what will happen at this point."

It didn't seem like there was much love lost between Jade and Patti Sue. She acted shocked, not sad. Hopefully, I could get her talking more about the murder. "So, this may seem odd, but as you might expect, having Patti Sue killed at the fashion show was not what the museum was hoping for. And the police seem to be on, what seems to me, the wrong track."

Jade leaned in. "It doesn't seem odd at all that you're looking into things. Everyone in town knows you've solved several crimes in the past year that had the police stumped."

Oh. I didn't realize it was such public knowledge.

"So, who do the police think did it?" Jade asked.

"Valerie Johnson," Cleo said.

Jade sat back, crossed her arms, and tapped one long, decorated nail on her arm. "I mean, Patti Sue might have offended her in some way. She could be horrid at times, but"—her face scrunched up—"I don't see it. Valerie hasn't lived here that long. I'd think you'd need more history with someone to be mad enough to murder them."

That made sense. And Jade herself certainly had history with Patti Sue.

"I tried to tell Libby what Patti Sue could be like." Cleo flipped her palms up, her fingers spread wide. "Maybe you can give her some examples, so she understands."

"Maybe?" Jade sniffed. "Try definitely. I mean, the last conversation we had, she was awful to me, simply awful. Telling me that if I didn't eat so many of those little candy bars, I wouldn't be so fat." She pointed to the bite-size candy bars. "Seriously, I let myself have one of those every afternoon at three o'clock. Never more. Those candy bars, which I read about doing online to help potential customers feel more at ease, are not the reason I'm overweight. Sadly, I'm one of those people who, no matter how hard I try, can't seem to be skinny."

"Everyone doesn't need to be skinny," Cleo said. "And

you look adorable. The nails, the outfit, and, of course, the hair." She grinned.

"You're very kind, but I tell you, working for Patti Sue was a challenge. When her husband owned the complex, I loved it here. But back then, Patti Sue worked at Grove University in Parking Services. Have you ever dealt with Parking Services?"

Cleo shuddered.

"You'll understand what I mean, then, when I tell you that she brought their 'customer is always wrong' attitude with her when she took over here. Some days I was mortified by how she treated the tenants and potential tenants."

"Really?" I asked. If any of our suspects was an unhappy renter, that might give them motive.

"Like I know on more than one occasion, Patti Sue told international students at Grove University that there were no vacancies when we had units open, simply because she said she"—Jade shifted her voice a few notes higher—"'didn't like those foreigners.'"

"Oh, that's awful. And illegal," I said. But none of our suspects were international students. "What else did she do?"

"Don't get me started on how many times she cheated renters out of their security deposits, claiming they did damage to the unit that she and I both knew was there before they moved in." Jade shook her head. "Generally, she tried to get every penny she could out of the tenants and put as little money as possible into the units. Like the time she was forced to replace the carpet before renting a second-floor unit because the former tenant stained it so badly. She put down the cheapest carpet with the thinnest possible pad, even though the carpet guy told her that if she'd spend a dollar more per yard, it would last way longer and be quieter for the tenant downstairs."

Other than having been a renter, I didn't know much about running an apartment complex, but to me, it seemed like Jade should have been the manager, not the assistant manager. She'd have done a better job than Patti Sue.

"It all adds up, and it's so different from when her husband, Arthur, ran the place." Jade blinked and gave a tight laugh. "Of course, I don't want you to think I hated her so much that I killed her. I would never kill anyone. I don't even kill bugs. I'm a vegetarian."

"I never meant to imply that you would." Although in my opinion, she seemed to have plenty of motive. "The question is, who could have killed her?"

Jade shifted in her seat and pressed her fingertips against her mouth.

Cleo leaned in. "Is there someone you think might have done it?"

"Well." Jade twisted her hands together, then leaned forward and lowered her voice. "I don't know for sure, of course, but I did see Chip Wasserman in the hallway before the murder. If I had to pick a suspect, I'd pick him."

Cleo tipped her head to one side. "Why? Does he live here?"

"Oh, no. I imagine as a professor, he lives in some big, fancy house. But he was in here last week yelling at Patti

Sue. I'd just come back from lunch and as soon as he saw me, he shut up real fast, like he was hiding something. Patti Sue, of course, ignored me when I later asked what was wrong."

"Now that's interesting," I said.

"He was definitely steamed," Jade said. "He was so upset that his face was red."

"Thank you." I stood. "I'd better get back to the museum, but I appreciate you talking with us. I'll let you know if we're able to reschedule the fashion show, and I'll look into Chip."

As soon as I got into Cleo's car, I sent Sam a text asking if there was a way we could talk to Chip.

I'd just gotten seated back at my desk at the museum when he called.

"Libby?"

Warmth swirled through my chest at the sound of his voice.

"Hi, Sam."

"There's a science event tonight, an open-air lecture where the public is invited. Chip is one of three speakers. If you're up for it, we could try to catch him as he's leaving the event. I've got to oversee a lab until seven, but I could pick you up at seven fifteen and drive you to campus."

"That would be great!"

"Since it's outside, Bella could come too. I bet she'd love walking on the green and meeting students."

"You know she would. It sounds perfect. We'll both be ready."

Excellent. With luck, Sam and I would be able to learn why Chip had been so angry with Patti Sue and—if we were skillful—be able to judge whether he might have been the killer.

Chapter Seven

"WE'LL HAVE to go a couple of blocks that way." Sam pointed as he climbed out of his car that evening. "Even at night, my permit only allows me to park in certain lots."

I stepped out of the car, opened the back door for Bella, and hooked on her leash. "It's such a lovely evening that a walk sounds great."

After six, when the sun had dropped low on the horizon, the temperatures cooled. It was still in the mid-eighties, but the humidity wasn't too bad, and Grove University was lovely, hitting the college campus aesthetic dead on. Tall trees shaded walkways between ivy-covered red-brick buildings.

Students wandered the college green in pairs or small groups, and several walked over when they saw Bella.

She greeted each student like a long-lost friend, nuzzling their legs, soaking up their attention, and even rolling on her back to get her tummy scratched by one young man.

"What a great dog," he said as he stood back up.

I beamed at him. "Thanks."

He gave Bella one final pat and headed off down a side path.

Sam and I continued on. Every so often, he waved at a colleague, and I even saw someone I knew, Sam's boss's wife, Dallas McAllister. I'd met her at a campus function in the spring.

Soon, Sam pointed out the open-air amphitheater ahead. "That's where the lecture is being given. Let's approach it from the back and see if the lecture's about done."

We found a spot near the amphitheater under a tree, and, although in the distance I could hear the Grove University marching band practicing, we could also hear Chip finishing up.

He announced the next lecture in the series and ran through a list of ways students could investigate careers in the sciences, which gave me time to study him.

He was of average height, built like a long-distance runner, and had sandy brown hair and a beard. He wore small, round glasses, and, although he was engaging as a speaker, there was something about the way he carried himself that made me think he had quite an ego.

Apparently, though, I was either wrong or being a multi-millionaire was enough to impress even Professor Wasserman, because he slid his notes into a messenger bag and strode right over when Sam waved to him. "Sam, great to see you."

"Chip, this is Libby Ballard." Sam angled his head toward me. "She runs the local history museum."

He shook my hand. "I remember you from Saturday. I was at the historical fashion show with my wife. Were the two of you here for the lecture tonight?"

"No," Sam said. "We wanted to talk with you. Since that murder took place at her event, Libby's eager for the killer to be caught."

Chip's eyes narrowed, and he nodded.

Bella walked closer to him and angled her head as if she expected to have her ears scratched.

Chip scowled at her, hitched his messenger bag higher on his shoulder, and crossed his arms over his chest.

He moved down another notch in my estimation.

I tugged on Bella's leash, pulling her back closer to me, and ran a hand down the back of her neck, reassuring her that she was loved. "I know it's a long shot," I said to Chip, "but one of my team remembered you had gone down the hall to take a phone call near the time of the murder. I wondered if you saw anything."

"Oh, yeah." Chip pointed at me. "You're the woman who likes to play detective."

Wow. Two people commenting on my sleuthing in one day.

But the other one didn't sound so condescending.

I wasn't going to be stopped by his attitude. "That's me. Did you notice anyone acting oddly?"

He ran a hand over the back of his neck. "No. I didn't even know the woman who was killed."

"That's strange." I knew I should tread lightly, but I couldn't let the guy flat-out lie to me. "I talked with someone who heard you have a big argument with her at Hartley Road Apartments."

"I—I—" He sputtered, then recovered his composure and peered down his nose at me. "I may have spoken with her once, but we weren't well acquainted, certainly not enough for me to have a reason to kill her if that's what you're implying."

"So why were you angry with her?" Sam asked calmly.

Chip's body tensed. He glanced at me, then at Sam, and then the tightness in his shoulders eased. "Okay, okay, I'll tell you the whole story." He motioned for us to walk with him away from the amphitheater to a spot under a large oak.

Sam reached over and squeezed my hand as we followed Chip.

Once under the tree, Chip stopped and turned to face us. "It's because of my research. I'm sure you'll understand, Sam."

I ignored the implication that I might not have enough brain cells to follow the conversation and waited for him to explain.

"I need to hire a new lab manager to oversee my research projects. Last week, a woman came into town to interview. She was the perfect candidate but was reluctant to move to such a small town. Thinking of how charming Dogwood Springs is and how she might be impressed by the low cost of living, I encouraged her to drive around and visit some apartment complexes."

"That's pretty much standard practice, right?" Sam said.

"Yeah," Chip said. "It usually works. But unfortunately, this woman visited Hartley Road Apartments. I'll admit, she didn't look like the typical person you'd meet here in Dogwood Springs. Tattoos up and down both arms and lots of piercings. But none of that affected her brain or her training."

I had to give him credit for that, at least. Maybe he wasn't a sexist, just more of an intellectual snob.

"Anyway," he continued, "Patti Sue was so rude and judgmental that the candidate took an offer from another university, thinking she was representative of the town. So, you see why I didn't mention getting angry with her. I was mad, but it wasn't enough to kill someone over."

Sam tipped his head in acknowledgment.

"Besides, I told the police who they should be investigating," Chip said.

"Who?" Sam and I asked.

"Gene Harrison, Patti Sue's brother-in-law. With her dead, I'm pretty sure he'll inherit that apartment complex."

"He will?" I rested my weight back on my heels. "Patti Sue and her husband didn't have children?"

"Not according to my wife." Chip edged back a step. "Speaking of my wife, I'd better get home. See you around campus, Sam. Good luck with your investigation, Libby."

He waved and walked away.

I turned to Sam. "What do you think?"

"It sounds like Gene had a much stronger motive than Chip," he said as we began walking back toward his car.

"I agree, assuming Chip is telling the truth. I think I need to talk to Gene next."

~

After Sam dropped Bella and me back home that night, I messaged Alice and Cleo, hoping one of them might know Gene.

Sure enough, Alice and her husband had used Gene's plumbing services for years. A quick phone call and she'd even learned Gene would be watching the Hartley Road Apartments office in the middle of the day the next day when Jade had a dentist appointment.

Sometimes it shocked me that anyone dared to commit a crime in Dogwood Springs. Having grown up in Columbus, Ohio, I was still frequently surprised by how little privacy there was in a small town. It wasn't so much that people were nosy, but that the town was so interwoven that even if someone only knew one part of a story, they probably had lunch with someone who knew the rest.

Which worked out well for me if I was trying to find a killer.

Alice offered to pick me up at lunch the next day so we could go talk to Gene.

Zeke hadn't started school yet and would be at a friend's house two blocks from my place, so he agreed to stop by my apartment at lunch to let Bella out.

I spent the rest of the evening working on a crossword, discussing some of the trickier clues with Bella, and listening to classic rock. I might be an anomaly among people my age, but I preferred music from the 1970s over more recent music. A song by The Who, the Eagles, or Jackson Browne had more character, at least in my opinion.

Eventually, I went to bed, eager to talk to Gene the following day.

It was a good thing we made plans ahead of time, because the next morning, I was swamped at the museum. Two volunteers failed to show up, and a potential donor unexpectedly stopped by wanting a personal tour. Then a pair of four-year-old twins wandered away from their mother while she was tending to their two-year-old sister. The poor woman was frantic.

I don't think I ever would have found the little stinkers, who managed to hide all the way up in the attic, except for the fact that I heard them giggling.

I had just reunited them with their very apologetic mother when my phone dinged with a text in my pocket. Alice was in the museum parking lot, ready to drive us over to talk to Gene. I hurried out the back door and climbed into her white SUV. My lunch, which I had hoped to eat early, would have to wait.

I sank into the front passenger seat and filled her in on my morning.

Alice, whose daughter had twins near the same age, was full of compassion for the young mom. Since I was still sweating from racing all over the building, my sympathy was more limited.

By the time we arrived at Hartley Road Apartments, Alice and I had a plan for how to talk to Gene, and I had cooled off.

Inside the office, a small, wiry man with white hair and a white beard sat at the same desk where Jade had been when Cleo and I had talked with her. Instead of his plumbing uniform, he wore a short-sleeved blue dress shirt and tan pants. He gave us a tired smile, exposing the fact that one of his yellowed front teeth sat at an odd angle. "Alice, how nice to see you."

Alice introduced me, mentioning my connection to the museum.

I said hello and waited for her to proceed as we'd planned. She expressed her condolences on his loss, then shifted the topic. "Libby's concerned that the police are on the wrong track in identifying Patti Sue's killer, and she's been asking around. She heard something disturbing, and I thought we should talk to you in person."

Gene pointed to the two chairs across from his desk, and we sat down.

"I was told," I said, "that at Patti Sue's death, as her brother-in-law, you inherit these apartments." I hesitated, not sure I should outright accuse the man of murder.

His chin jutted out like the head of a banty rooster. "Durn it, are people saying I killed her to get this place? I never liked the woman, and I will inherit the business, but I wouldn't kill for it."

Alice laid a hand over her collarbone. "I, for one, don't see you as a murderer. You can understand why people might wonder, though. These apartments must be quite profitable."

Her words calmed him, and his defensiveness melted away. "I guess ... I mean, me and the wife ... Geez, it's hard to believe she's been gone three years now." He shook his head rapidly as if pushing away a painful memory. "It was bad enough, losing her, but then, two years ago, I lost my brother, Arthur, as well."

"I'm so sorry," Alice said.

"That must have been hard," I added.

His face tensed and he gave an almost imperceptible nod. "After our parents died when I was fourteen, he raised me."

A wave of guilt washed through me. This poor man was still grieving two huge losses, and here I was, implying he might be a murderer. He could be, but I felt bad adding to his pain.

Gene straightened in his chair. "Anyway, me and the wife never had kids, and neither did Arthur and Patti Sue. So, it is true. I will inherit this place." He surveyed the room without a flicker of interest. "But I made good money over the years as a plumber and never wanted anything fancy. Plus, we saved every month and made a few decent investments." He shrugged. "Most people don't understand, but I don't want fancy new cars or big vacations. I just want to drive my old truck out to the river and go fishing."

"I can see that," Alice said. "You understand what's important in life, and it's not possessions."

He shot Alice a look of gratitude. "I've been thinking of retirement, trying to find someone qualified to take over my business. Don't worry," he added quickly. "I won't retire until I can leave things in capable hands. I've got a responsibility to people like you who've been my clients all these years. As for those apartments, until I can sell them, they'll simply be one more thing to deal with when I'd rather be out at the river."

"Thinking of things from another angle," I said. "You must have known Patti Sue well. Can you think of anyone who would have wanted to kill her?"

Gene stared off to one side, pursed his lips, then looked back at us. "Nah, nobody in particular. I mean, the woman made a lot of people mad, but I can't think of anyone who hated her more than the rest."

I picked up my purse. "Thank you for talking with us."

As we left the office, Alice and I again offered our condolences on the loss of his sister-in-law, but I had a feeling they fell on deaf ears. Gene wasn't mourning the loss of Patti Sue. He was still mourning his wife and brother.

I climbed back into Alice's SUV and blew out a long breath. I'd talked to three suspects and had no clue who the killer might be. None of them seemed likely.

There was a chance, though, I was being too trusting.

"Alice, do you still have that friend who's a real estate agent?"

"I do." She pulled out of the apartment complex and onto Hartley Road.

"Do you think you could check to see what this complex might be worth? And see if Gene has been talking to anyone about listing it? You never know, he might have met with an agent already and seemed really eager for the money from the sale."

"My friend's out of town on vacation for a few days, but I'll text her," Alice agreed. "I don't see Gene as a killer, though."

"I don't either, but we've got to check every angle. I just don't know what angle to check next and—"

My phone dinged with a text.

Imani Jones
Libby! I think I might have a clue to help you find the killer!

Chapter Eight

ONCE I WAS BACK at the museum, I stopped in my office to put my purse in my desk.

Imani, who must have heard me come up the back stairs, stuck her head in my office doorway.

"Tell me what you've learned." I sat down and gestured to the chair across from my desk.

She grinned and hurried into the room to sit across from me. "After all that mess with the missing twins, I was talking with Bethany, that volunteer who often helps Rodney, and she mentioned that she'd heard Noreen and Patti Sue arguing. Apparently, Noreen had wanted to wear the yellow suit her aunt loaned to the fashion show."

"Why didn't she say so?" I'd tried really hard to make all the volunteer models happy with what they wore.

"I'm not exactly sure. It seems like she was going to, but when you stepped out of the room to check on something else, Patti Sue insisted that she be the one to wear it."

Noreen was taller than Patti Sue, but she could easily have worn the suit from her aunt. Patti Sue would have needed higher heels to wear the Gibson Girl dress, but she and Noreen could have switched. They were both slender. I ran a hand through my hair. I loved historic garments, but the fashion show had been nothing but trouble. Even trouble I'd been unaware of.

"Here's the interesting part," Imani said. "At one point in the squabble, while you were out of the room, it seemed like Noreen was going to argue more. Then her eyes narrowed sharply, and she acquiesced. So maybe, maybe, she decided that she'd let Patti Sue wear the suit, but that she'd make sure Patti Sue didn't enjoy it."

"That seems like a huge leap." I couldn't see someone committing murder simply because they didn't get to wear a certain outfit in a small-town special event.

"Yeah, that's what I thought," Imani said. "But apparently the expression on Noreen's face was something to see. Bethany said she'd never seen anyone look more like they were planning something sneaky."

"I guess it couldn't hurt to have a chat with Noreen."

"That's what I thought you'd say." Imani popped up out of her chair. "I've got to dash, but I sure hope you find someone else for the police to consider instead of Valerie. I just can't imagine her as a murderer."

She hurried out of my office, and I gathered up three checks we'd received in the mail. The bank's website was down, so I filled out a deposit slip and stepped out onto Main Street to walk to the bank. I was passing the Dogwood

Springs Bakery when Valerie came out, holding a paper bag marked with the bakery's logo. The intoxicating aroma of fresh cookies wafted out of the shop.

"Hi, Valerie. Did you get something yummy?"

"A giant chocolate brownie." Her eyes lit but then clouded. "Have you made any progress finding another possible suspect for the murder? I talked with Detective Harper again recently, and he still thinks I killed Patti Sue. He just can't prove it."

"No progress yet. I'm hoping to talk with Noreen soon. Someone mentioned something that made her seem suspicious."

Valerie's face brightened. "I don't know Noreen very well, but talking with her should be easy. She's right inside." She pointed to the bakery.

"She is?" I had more than half an hour before the bank closed. Ordinarily, I'd rather interview a suspect with a friend, but a conversation in the bakery in the late afternoon sure seemed safe. I took a step toward the door.

"Fingers crossed," Valerie said.

"I'll let you know if I learn anything." I gave Valerie a supportive smile and stepped into the bakery.

The bell over the door jingled, and a blast of cold air from the air conditioner blew down on me as I entered the bakery. The owner waved and pointed to a row of shortbread cookies in the case.

I rubbed my hands together in anticipation.

First, though, I needed to talk to Noreen.

She was second in line, and I took my place behind her.

Her dark hair was pulled back in a very short ponytail, and she wore ice-blue scrubs. If I had to guess, I'd say she'd gotten off work at the hospital at three and come downtown to run errands.

"Noreen, I'm glad to see you," I said. "I wanted to ask you something."

"Oh?" She turned, and her bright-red, dangling ladybug earrings bounced back and forth.

"Someone told me you wanted to wear your aunt's 1940s suit in the fashion show. I feel terrible. I didn't know."

"That's okay," she said gently. "It wouldn't have mattered anyway. No one got to see the show."

I tipped my head in acknowledgment. "True. It turned out to be quite a day."

The two of us stood silent for a moment.

"How come you didn't tell me you wanted to wear it?" I asked.

"I hate to say it after the tragedy, but ..." She made an awkward gesture with her hands. "Patti Sue was just so pushy. And I was wearing shorts the day we decided who would wear which dress, and she made some comment about my ankles being kind of thick, which I've always been rather self-conscious about. So, when she said I should wear a dress that was longer to hide them, I ... I sort of agreed with her."

"I'm sorry she was so rude to you."

Noreen's mouth twisted to one side. "Yeah, as soon as I'd agreed that she could wear that suit, I started getting mad. She always got what she wanted, no matter how it made other people feel."

"That would make me mad too. After all, the suit belonged to your aunt."

"I thought about saying I'd changed my mind and arguing with her, but then I ... I thought about doing something else instead." She edged back a step.

Dread welled up inside me. "What was that?" I asked quietly. I wanted to find the person who killed Patti Sue, but I suddenly realized I didn't want that person to be Noreen. She'd been a volunteer at the museum since right after Christmas, and I liked her.

"Well," she continued slowly. "I have these two nephews that are always playing practical jokes on each other. I knew they had itching powder, and I had this idea pop into my head that when she wasn't looking, I could sprinkle itching powder all over the inside of that yellow suit." Noreen gave a nervous giggle.

I let out a silent sigh. She wasn't a killer. That guilty expression Bethany had seen hadn't been Noreen planning a murder. She'd been planning a practical joke. "But I saw Patti Sue before the show. She didn't seem uncomfortable."

"In the end, I chickened out," Noreen said. "I almost think all I needed was the image of her twisting and scratching to feel better. I didn't need to act on the idea. And when I pictured myself wearing that lemon yellow color, I knew I'd be washed out. Then you offered me that Gibson

Girl dress to wear. It's such a pretty shade of royal blue. Patti Sue's coloring wasn't much different from mine, so I decided to skip the itching powder and simply enjoy how pale and pasty Patti Sue would look in lemon yellow."

"Blue probably would be a better color on both of you." I knew all too well how the wrong color could make my own normally pale skin appear even paler. "I guess in the end, it didn't matter for Patti Sue."

"No. I never dreamed she'd ..." Noreen shook her head. "No matter how mean and pushy she was, she didn't deserve to be strangled."

The woman in line ahead of Noreen took her bag of treats and moved aside.

Noreen stepped forward and ordered two dozen cookies, divided among five different flavors, which she said were treats for a co-worker's birthday celebration the next day.

The bakery owner went to the back to get more of one variety, and I cleared my throat.

Noreen turned back to face me.

"The police think the killer was Valerie, but I find that hard to believe," I said.

Noreen shifted her weight from one foot to the other and glanced off to one side.

"Do you have someone you suspect?"

"I hate to name names ... but I have wondered if Edna did it."

"Edna?" Of all the people we had identified as having the opportunity to kill Patti Sue, Edna seemed like the meekest of the lot.

Noreen tucked a wisp of hair behind one ear. "I heard a rumor that several years ago, back when Edna's husband was still alive, he and Patti Sue had something going on. I could imagine Patti Sue making some nasty comment about that and Edna—even though she's an incredibly nice woman—just losing it."

"It's not a bad theory." And totally new information to me. "I'll give it some thought. Thanks for talking with me, Noreen."

"No problem. And seriously, Libby?" Her face tensed up. "I value the historical objects at the museum. I never would have really used the itching powder. You don't need to worry about me being a bad volunteer."

"I understand, Noreen. Thinking about it was only a way to blow off steam."

Her features relaxed. "That's it exactly. Thank you for being so understanding."

"I appreciate all you do to help the museum. Have a good evening."

She reached over and squeezed my arm. "Thank you." Then she stepped up to the cash register to pay for her cookies.

I bought a freshly baked shortbread cookie to take home, then hurried to the bank, thinking about what Noreen had said and how she'd behaved. Someone who felt that guilty about considering a practical joke didn't strike me as a murderer.

Not nearly as likely as a woman whose husband had had an affair with Patti Sue.

Chapter Nine

AS SOON AS I got home, Bella galloped into the kitchen, sat down in front of the cabinet where I stored the dog food, and gave it a pointed stare.

"Yes, you're right, I'm a little late. It's already twenty-five past five." I laughed and added kibble to her bowl, topped it with some of the canned food she adored, and picked up her water bowl to rinse it and refill it.

I'd barely set down her water when Sam called. "Do you have dinner plans?" he asked.

"No. I was about to scrounge in the refrigerator for some leftovers."

"You know that antique bookcase my decorator recently added to the entryway of my house?"

"I remember it." It was a beautiful piece.

"I've found something odd about it, and I wondered if you'd like to come over. We could order a pizza, and you could take a peek." His voice held a note of excitement, almost as if he was trying to keep from spilling a surprise.

"Sure. I can be there in fifteen minutes. Bella's just eating her dinner, but ..." I looked down at her bowl, which was already empty. "Nope. She's done. See you soon."

I ran into my bedroom, changed into shorts and a cute T-shirt, and grabbed my purse. "Come on, Bella. Let's take a ride in the car to go see Sam. He says he's found something odd about his antique bookcase."

Bella nudged her leash off its hook on the kitchen wall. If I had to guess, I'd say she understood at least three of my words: *ride, car,* and *Sam.* Within less than a minute we were pulling out of the driveway.

Unless someone went through downtown, which sometimes got clogged with tourists, Dogwood Springs didn't have traffic to speak of, especially not when I compared it to Philadelphia, where I used to live.

Today, of all the luck, even though I cut through some side roads to avoid Main Street, I managed to hit every red light. Maybe it was because it was the end of the workday, or maybe I noticed the delays more because Sam had piqued my curiosity.

Finally, though, I crossed Cedar Creek and neared the turn for Ashlington.

As always, the sight of the house brought a lightness to my chest. When I was a child and came to Ashlington with my parents, that happy feeling had been triggered by the knowledge that I'd be getting lots of my grandma's hugs and playing cards with my grandpa. These days, it was thoughts of Sam—fun, handsome, sexy Sam—that made me smile when I saw Ashlington.

The sprawling peach Victorian sat on a hill, glowing in the late afternoon sun. Two-and-a-half stories tall, it featured two chimneys, a wide, rounded front porch with a matching rounded balcony above, gingerbread details, and —best of all—a turret.

Much as I loved the place, though, I could understand why my mom's oldest sister had sold it. The place was a money pit. It belonged with someone like Sam who had plenty of cash to pour into upkeep. He'd done several necessary repairs, as well as some long-overdue remodeling to the kitchen and bathrooms, turning it into quite the showplace.

I pulled up the long driveway, and Sam stepped out onto the porch, waving. He had on one of those outfits that on the surface was so ordinary, tan shorts and a navy polo. It was only after I'd dated him a while that I'd learned to recognize from how soft the shirts were and how well the clothes fit that it was one of the outfits he'd bought in California—brands where even a simple T-shirt could cost $300. Needless to say, he looked great.

Bella gave a loud woof when she spotted him. When I opened her door, she raced up the porch steps to greet him, ran back down the steps, and then did a quick lap around his enormous front yard.

I reached back into the car, slid the straps of my purse

over my shoulder, and climbed the porch steps. "Okay, I'm hooked. I want to see what you found!"

Sam laughed, drew me in for a quick kiss, and opened the front door. "After you."

I called Bella, and the three of us went inside with Bella panting.

"See if you notice anything unusual about the bookcase. I'll get Bella some water in the kitchen." He clapped his hand against his thigh. "C'mon girl."

The two of them headed down the hall and I turned toward the bookcase.

The piece was about eight feet tall and four feet wide with curved sides and beautifully matched wood. The base was solid, and the upper portion had front shelves behind glass doors and small, curved, open shelves on both of the rounded sides.

A gorgeous piece of furniture, but nothing struck me as unusual.

"I knew this thing had secrets," Sam said when he returned. He pushed on a piece of molding, which made a section pop out on one of the curved sides of what had looked like a solid base. He rotated it like a lazy Susan, revealing a small, hidden shelf.

"How cool!"

"According to my interior designer, this is where the original owner probably stashed his best whiskey. There's a matching compartment on the other side, but the mechanism that rotates it is broken."

"Isn't that neat?" I turned the section back and the outer shell slid into place, hiding the storage spot entirely.

"This afternoon, I happened to notice that the bottom shelf on each of the side bookshelf sections is slightly taller than the shelves above it."

"You're right. It is." I'd totally missed that and now studied the shelves more closely.

"It isn't like the space for books is taller. There is just more wood above and below those bottom side shelves. I got to thinking that the bookcase already had two secret compartments. I wondered if it had more."

"And you found one?"

Sam grinned. "Watch."

He removed the six books from the lowest shelf on the right side and, pressing outward on both sides to gain hold, he pulled forward a box that fit exactly into the shelf space. The box was open on one side, the side where the books had been stored.

Then he reached behind where the box had been and pulled out a smaller wooden box that, although dove-tailed, was less highly finished than the rest of the cabinet.

I drew in a sharp breath. "A secret storage compartment."

I'd read articles about furniture with hidden compartments, so popular before banks had safety deposit boxes. Having Sam find one in person was as exciting as some of the things on *Antiques Roadshow*.

"It was empty," Sam said. "Except for a dead spider."

I shuddered. Try as I might, I couldn't get past my aversion to spiders.

Bella came over and gave the box several sniffs, clearly enjoying its slightly musty smell.

"So, I figured that since the piece is symmetrical, there had to be another compartment on the other side. That's when I stopped and called you."

I stared at him in disbelief. "You mean you haven't looked?"

"Nope. You're the historian. I thought you should have the honors."

If I hadn't already been in love with Sam Collins, that would have done it right there. After all, the cabinet belonged to him. The curiosity must have been nearly impossible to resist.

I pulled him into a tight hug. "Thank you!" I whispered. "You are so incredibly sweet to wait and let me open the other side."

He kissed the top of my head, then stepped back. "Let's hunt for the matching dead spider!" He laughed, and I knew that if I did find a spider, dead or alive, he'd scoop it up and take it outside without me even asking.

I removed the books from the lowest shelf on the left side. There was no lip that stuck out to grab onto, so I pushed my hands out on each side of the section's walls, trying to get it to slip out.

Nothing happened.

"I had to pull pretty hard," Sam said. "It was stuck."

That made sense. The piece was old and had likely been

damaged by humidity. I tugged again and this time, an inner box slid out about a quarter of an inch. Not much, but enough for me to grasp it on each side. I pulled it out and saw, like on the right side, a secret box hidden behind it.

My heart rate sped up. Sure, most likely the compartment was empty, like the one on the other side. Or maybe it, too, held a spider. But there was a chance something had been hidden there by a previous owner.

I pulled out the secret box, and Sam and I peered inside.

Laying flat on the bottom of the box was a yellowed envelope addressed in a thin, wobbly hand to "My Darling Daughter."

Adrenaline shot through me, but I didn't say a word, simply gazed up at Sam.

"C'mon." He pulled the letter out of the box, handed it to me, and slid the secret box and the false liner back into place. "Let's read it!" He led the way into his living room.

We sat on his couch with Bella beside us, watching intently, and I lifted the envelope flap enough to wriggle a finger underneath. A second later, I pulled out a yellowed sheet of typing paper.

The two of us leaned in to read it.

My Darling Daughter,

My strength is fading fast, and although I know you are on your way, I fear I may pass away while you are traveling. I cannot die without telling you my secret.

If you are reading this, I didn't get to see you one last time as I had hoped. However, I knew if I hid a note in the compartment where I used to hide candy when you were a girl, you would find it.

Heavens, my heart is pounding even thinking of telling you this. Please forgive me for keeping it from you for so long.

Even now, in the 1960s, it is difficult for me to admit it, but my entire life was based on a lie.

I promise you that I did not begin living a life based on falsehoods easily, and I certainly did not lie to you without considerable pain. I hope you will believe me when I say that I would never have gone down this path except for very difficult circumstances.

The best way for you to understand would be if you would read my diary from when I first came to town. I have hidden it behind a loose brick in the fireplace. If you look on the third row of bricks up from the bottom near the right side of the fireplace, you will find it. The brick is a slightly darker shade than the ones next to it.

I pray you will find the diary, read it, and—once you understand the situation I was in—forgive me.

Please know that being your mom was my greatest pride and joy and that I wish you every happiness life can bring.

Always, always remember that I love you with all of my heart.

Please forgive me.

Mom

"Oh, this poor woman." I ran a finger over the letter. "So afraid that her daughter might not forgive her. I really hope the daughter arrived in time, and that the mother was able to talk with her and die at peace."

"I don't think that happened," Sam said. "The daughter would have removed the letter from the bookcase."

My heart sank. He was right. "And she would have kept it if she found it. So, the mother died, and, despite what she expected, her daughter never read this letter."

Sam sat up taller. "How many times do people go around trying each brick on their fireplace to see if it pulls out?"

I thought of my own fireplace, back on Elm Street. "Um, never."

"Which means the diary could still be there," Sam said. "We could find it and learn what the big secret was."

Bella must have sensed the excitement in his voice because she let out two loud barks and wriggled between us.

I scratched her ears. "The bookcase could have come from a house out in Oregon or somewhere equally far away. And the house with the hidden diary could have been demolished or even burned down. But maybe ..."

"Maybe it's another historical mystery for us to try to solve. Exactly like you predicted."

When I'd first met Sam, he'd found a mysterious painting in the attic of Ashlington. It took a while, but we'd eventually learned that the painting, which he'd later donated to the museum, was a valuable work by a noted American artist. After even more historical sleuthing, we'd learned why a young woman had been painted out of the picture by a later, less talented artist and found the woman's connection to Dogwood Springs.

Since then, I'd been secretly hoping we might find another historical mystery to puzzle out together. What if this letter was the beginning of just such a mystery?

I shook my head in wonder. "We've got to talk to your interior designer. We need to know where this piece came from—"

"So we can try to find the right fireplace and find the diary," Sam said. "Oh, man, are we ever going to have a story to tell my parents when they visit on Saturday."

"Yeah," I agreed, but even to my own ears, my voice sounded flat.

"You're not still nervous about meeting Mom and Dad, are you?"

"A little," I admitted.

"Libby, you have nothing to worry about. They're going to love you. It will be just as nice as when I got to meet your parents."

"I hope so." I didn't want to dwell on my fears, so I shifted the conversation back to our discovery. "You should call your interior designer."

Sam tried but got no answer.

We read the letter again, searching for more clues, but didn't find any beyond the mention of the diary and the implication that the letter must have been hidden in the 1960s.

Eventually, we got hungry and ordered a pizza. While we waited, I sent a quick text to Alice, Cleo, and Zeke. I let them know what we'd found, and Alice and I made plans to try to talk to Edna the next day at lunch.

After our pizza, Sam and I stayed up late, watching a movie and eating Minnesota's Pride ice cream, a brand that one day soon was bringing out a flavor tied to Dogwood Springs.

After the credits rolled, I nudged a snoring Bella with my toe. "We've got to head home girl."

She slowly stretched and shook herself all over, making her tags jingle.

Sam stood and walked me to the door.

We passed the bookcase, and the earlier events of the evening came flooding back into my memory, pushing out the story from the movie.

"Hey." I slid an arm around his waist. "Thanks again for waiting and letting me open the second compartment. That was so nice of you."

He shrugged. "It was no big deal."

"It was. And it was really special that you realized how much it would mean to me."

"I may not always manage, but I try to pay attention to what matters to you." He ran his fingertips down the side of my face, then cupped the back of my head with his hand. "I love you, Libby."

Warmth filled my chest, and I gazed up at him. "I love you too."

And he drew me closer and kissed me.

Chapter Ten

THE NEXT MORNING, I dashed home at eleven fifteen to let Bella out, planning to go back to the museum and eat my own lunch while I dealt with some administrative tasks. But once I walked back into the museum, I got delayed by a question from a volunteer. I had a meeting at one, so, after a quick text exchange, I brought my tuna salad sandwich and apple along while Alice drove us to Edna's house.

"Thanks for not minding that I'm eating in your car," I said as I climbed into her luxury SUV.

Alice waved my concern aside. "Those two grandsons of mine often have snacks in the car. I take it in and have it washed and vacuumed once a week."

Ah. That explained why it was always spotless. "Where are we headed?" I asked.

"Edna lives on Pleasant View Drive."

"What part of town is that?" Dogwood Springs wasn't

that big, but I'd lived here less than eighteen months. I hadn't been to all the residential areas yet.

"It's near the university. Very attractive homes, built in the 1980s. Edna's husband was a geology professor, but he passed away about ten years ago."

As always, Alice was a treasure trove of information about Dogwood Springs residents. All I'd known about Edna was that she was a quiet, reliable, highly intelligent volunteer who'd retired from working at an insurance company. In time, hopefully, I'd know my volunteers better.

A few minutes later, Alice pulled into the driveway of a pretty, gray, two-story home with pots of pink geraniums on the porch. "That's Patti Sue's." She pointed next door at a larger white house in a similar style.

We got out, followed a path lined with gray slate pavers, and climbed stone steps to a large wooden front porch.

Edna opened the door almost the minute we knocked. Her long grayish-blond hair was pulled back in a loose braid, and she wore a pink T-shirt and navy knit pants. "Libby, Alice, please come in." She wore no visible makeup, but the bright frame of her glasses drew attention to her cornflower blue eyes.

We followed her into a living room done in blues and greens. A collection of mineral specimens stood proudly on a side table, a grandfather clock ticked along the far wall, and the faint smell of potpourri filled the air.

Edna led us to a seating area where a pitcher of iced tea and three glasses were waiting.

Alice and I readily agreed to tea, and after Edna poured,

I took a sip, savoring the rich flavor of a high-quality, freshly brewed glass of iced tea.

"It's so nice to have you all visit," Edna said. "It makes me think of Don Felding, who used to bring Bella over once a week when he and I played chess."

"You know Bella?" Don Felding had been Bella's previous owner. When he'd died, I'd ended up with his apartment and his dog.

"I do indeed. She's such a sweet dog," Edna said. "How can I help you today?"

"I don't know if you're aware," Alice said, "but the police suspect Valerie Johnson of killing Patti Sue."

Edna sat back in her chair. "Does she have a motive?" Her voice held a note of skepticism.

"None." I sat my glass on a coaster on an end table. "Which is why I'm hoping you can help us. Alice says you lived next door to Patti Sue for many years. Maybe you can tell us something about her that might help us figure out who the real killer is."

"What was she like as a neighbor?" Alice asked.

Edna's gaze shifted toward Alice, and she sat for a second, seemingly collecting her thoughts. "Honestly," she said at last, "from the day my husband and I moved in here more than forty years ago, I've loved all my neighbors. Except Patti Sue. She was … difficult."

"I did hear a rumor," I said slowly. "Something about your husband and—"

"Ah." Edna took a sip of her tea and set down the glass.

"I guess I should have expected that to resurface. That explains your visit."

I shifted in my chair.

"Well, I don't know if you'll believe me, but there was nothing to it." Edna stretched her shoulders and ran her hands down her thighs. "Never in a million years would I believe my Stan had an affair. He was as steady and solid as the igneous rocks he loved to collect. But Patti Sue ..." Edna shook her head.

"It was a lie?" Alice asked.

"I'm not sure how much Patti Sue believed it. She was an odd woman. Saw herself as the star of every interaction she had. So, if Stan politely waved at her years ago when he took out the trash, she could very well have believed he was madly in love with her."

"Wow. That sounds like she wasn't quite there mentally," I said. "I didn't pick up on that at all when we planned the fashion show."

"Oh, she was as sane as the next person." Edna gave a subtle shrug. "But pretty high on the narcissism scale. After her husband died, I think it fed her ego to think that there had been more to her past relationship with Stan than simply being neighbors. And to tell other people that."

"That would make me furious," I said.

Edna tipped her head to one side and gave me a half-smile. "I tried to keep in mind that she had some issues. I hoped other people understood that as well. If I had to guess, it all tied back to emotional wounds in her childhood."

"Oh? I didn't move to Dogwood Springs until I was an adult," Alice said. "What happened when Patti Sue was a child?"

"Even though Patti Sue and Bobbi Sue have similar features, they didn't have the same mother. Patti Sue's mother abandoned her and her dad when she was three. He remarried and had Bobbi Sue with his second wife."

"The names were the father's idea?" I asked.

"I think Sue was in honor of his mother." Edna took a long sip of tea. "I can imagine how her mother's abandonment might have given Patti Sue deep insecurities that came out in narcissistic tendencies, but that didn't make her any more pleasant to deal with. I'll even admit there were times when she rang my doorbell that I pretended not to be home. I figured if my car was in the garage, she couldn't know for sure, and there were days I didn't need her negative energy."

Hmmm. Those didn't seem like the words of a woman who would take such a vicious action as strangling Patti Sue. Oh, Edna certainly had reason to be angry with her neighbor, but she seemed above being drawn into Patti Sue's poison. And on the scale of how much a person was comfortable with conflict, Edna seemed like she was far at the conflict-avoidant end of the spectrum.

But maybe, even if she didn't seem like the killer, she could still help us solve this murder.

"You must have seen people come and go from Patti Sue's house," I said. "Possibly even overheard a conversation in the yard. Is there anyone that you think might have killed her?"

Again, Edna waited before she spoke, as if mulling over the exact phrasing she would use. "I didn't mention it when the police talked with me, but there is someone, based on gossip, who I would consider as a possible suspect."

"Oh?" I leaned in.

"Do you know Trent, who owns Green Thumb Gardens out on Hartley Road?" Edna asked.

Alice nodded.

I hadn't met Trent, but he was one of our suspects because he'd gone down the hall toward the bathrooms near the time of the murder.

Edna continued. "I was talking with a repair guy who was here a couple of weeks ago, and he told me that Patti Sue was pretty much responsible for Trent losing his previous business, Trent's Lawn Care."

"What did she do?" Alice asked.

"Have you ever put sod in?" Edna glanced at each of us, and we both shook our heads. "Well, after they put it down, you're supposed to water it every morning and evening for ten days or so, maybe two weeks. It might depend on the time of year ... Anyway, Trent put sod down after there was some sewer work done at the apartment complex, and he explained to Patti Sue that the watering was her responsibility."

"That makes sense," Alice said. "Like when I had a big shrub replaced, even though the landscape company did the digging and planted it, I was supposed to water it."

"Exactly," Edna agreed. "But Patti Sue didn't. When the grass all died because she neglected it, she blamed

Trent. And then she bad-mouthed his lawn-care business all over town. Most people take Patti Sue's nasty comments with a grain of salt, but I guess enough folks believed her that Trent's lawn care business went bankrupt."

Alice and I exchanged glances. She looked as shocked as I felt.

"I remember that happening," Alice said. "I never knew why."

"I think the only way he was able to open his new greenhouse was because his wife inherited some money," Edna explained.

"Wow," I said. "Driving a business into bankruptcy is a pretty good motive for murder."

"That's what I thought. I mean"—Edna spread her hands wide—"it's only speculation on my part. But at least it gives Trent some motive. And I spent quite a bit of time talking with Valerie when we were working on the fashion show. She seemed to get along as well as anyone with Patti Sue. I didn't detect any animosity that would have led her to commit murder."

"That was my impression as well." And the more I spoke with this quiet woman who thought about things deeply, the less I considered her a possible suspect. "I appreciate your thoughts and your delicious iced tea, but I guess we'd better be going. I need to get back to the museum."

Edna walked us to the front door and thanked us for stopping by.

Alice and I returned to her SUV, and I pulled an apple

out of my lunch bag, polished it with a paper napkin I'd packed, and then took a bite.

"I can't believe I've never heard any of that," Alice said. "I thought I was up on all the gossip, especially anything to do with area garden centers. Apparently not."

"You can't hear *all* the gossip." I smiled at her. "After all, most of the time you spend volunteering, you're actually working. Which places like the museum really appreciate," I added.

"Oh, Libby, you're sweet." Alice turned onto Main Street. "Trent does sound like someone we should talk to, though."

"I agree. His motive is the strongest we've heard so far. Far stronger than Edna's. Do you know Trent well enough to want to go with me to talk with him after I get off work?"

Alice shook her head. "I can't. I'm watching my grandsons, but I don't want you going by yourself. If Trent is capable of strangling Patti Sue and you're alone with him in the shop, what's to keep him from whacking you over the head with a shovel?"

I winced. "Good point. Hold on." I sent a quick text to Cleo, Sam, and Zeke.

Cleo was booked at the salon until nearly eight that evening. Zeke had already made plans with Zoe. But Sam was free and offered to pick me up once I'd had a chance to feed Bella after work.

"All set," I told Alice. "Sam and I will talk to Trent tonight." And even though I wasn't going alone, I would be on my guard.

Chapter Eleven

AT FIVE THIRTY THAT EVENING, Sam knocked on my kitchen door.

I let him in and chuckled as Bella wolfed down the last bit of kibble in her bowl then raced to greet him, circling him repeatedly with her tail wagging at top speed. "I think Bella is glad to see you," I said.

"Only Bella?" Sam teased, and he leaned across Bella to kiss me.

"Uh, maybe she's not alone," I said, doing my best to fake nonchalance.

He grinned as if he saw right through me. "Are you and Bella ready to go?"

"I am. But I checked the website for Green Thumb Gardens. Pets are not welcome."

"So many places make a big deal these days about being pet friendly. You'd think a greenhouse would welcome them, but I guess it's their choice." He knelt to scratch

Bella's tummy while I refilled her water bowl and grabbed my purse.

After I told her that we wouldn't be gone long and that she was the best dog in the whole world, Sam and I set off in his blue Tesla.

It was only a ten-minute drive from my apartment to Green Thumb Gardens, which was located just past the apartment complex on Hartley Road that Patti Sue had owned.

The business was small compared to some I'd seen in the area, with only two greenhouses as wings off a main building. Once we went inside the shop, I realized that in addition to plants and garden tools, it carried stained glass, local pottery, and a collection of terrariums. Each terrarium had a different theme, including one labeled "No Place Like Gnome," which was absolutely delightful.

A young woman sat behind the counter, putting price tags on some ceramic pieces. Her bright orange T-shirt had a cute logo of a green thumb growing out of a flowerpot that I'd guess was designed by the same person who made the terrariums. It had the same note of whimsy.

"Hi." I walked up to her. "Is Trent around?"

She angled her head to the left. "Over in Greenhouse 1. He's unpacking daylilies."

I thanked her, and Sam and I walked through the pottery section and out a doorway that led to a covered walkway and into Greenhouse 1.

Inside the greenhouse, sunshine poured through the

plastic walls and ceiling, glinted off the glossy green leaves of hostas, and gave an extra radiance to the blossoms of pink and red mandevillas. The air smelled rich and earthy, and a giant exhaust fan whirred, attempting to keep the temperature cool enough for the plants in the sweltering Missouri summer.

At the far end of the enclosure, a man in jean shorts and the company T-shirt was unwrapping bare-root plants from a large cardboard box and planting them in individual pots. He had graying hair under a bright-orange ball cap, brown glasses, and a short, scruffy beard.

"Trent?" Sam asked.

"That's me." He set down the flowerpot he was holding and walked down the gravel path between tables of plants toward us.

Although Alice couldn't accompany us, she'd encouraged me to use her name to help start the conversation. I couldn't just walk up to a stranger and ask him if he was a murderer.

"Hi, Trent." I stepped closer. "My name is Libby Ballard, and I'm the director of the Dogwood Springs History Museum." I gestured toward Sam. "This is my friend, Sam Collins. I'm also good friends with Alice VanMeter. She said you might remember her."

Trent's face brightened and the deeply tanned skin around his eyes crinkled. "Sure. I know Alice. She's a great customer and one of the best gardeners in town."

"She does have some amazing plants," I agreed.

"So, what brings you in?" Trent asked. "I've got some

gorgeous new daylilies if you're interested. There's a new coral-colored variety that's supposed to be a real winner."

"Well ..." I shifted my weight from one foot to the other. "Actually, I'm not here about plants. I'm here about what happened to Patti Sue Harrison at the fashion show the museum hosted at the high school."

"Oh yeah," Trent said. "You're the person in charge. I was there with my wife."

"That's why I wanted to talk with you," I said. "You were seen near where Patti Sue was killed at about the time of the murder. And someone told me that you were a very likely suspect because of some business dealings you'd had with Patti Sue."

"I should have expected the good people of Dogwood Springs to put those two things together." His tone was sarcastic, but it held a note of humor, and his body language stayed relaxed.

Which was odd. I'd expected him to be defensive, even if he was innocent.

"There is some logic in the idea," Trent admitted. "But no real truth. I'm not a killer."

Not as much info as I'd hoped for, but at the moment I couldn't think how to get him to reveal more. "Maybe you saw the killer?"

"You said you work at the museum." His eyes narrowed. "Why are you asking? You're not a cop."

"No, I'm not. I'm sure you can understand, though, that since I'm the director of the museum, I'm highly motivated to get this situation resolved. As long as people think Patti

Sue might have been killed because of something related to the museum, attendance is abysmal. Think if someone was killed here at your greenhouse."

"That would be awful." Trent looked at me, then at Sam, and back at me. "Isn't what you're doing kind of dangerous?"

I angled my head in acknowledgment. "It could be, I guess, but I'm trying to be careful. Can you help me? Tell me anything you know about Patti Sue or anything you saw that day?"

"Well, first off," he said with a chuckle, "I want to clear up any suspicion you might have that I was the killer. I know a fishing expedition when I see one."

Busted.

"You've probably heard about the incident with the sod and how it destroyed my previous business. Patti Sue was an irresponsible idiot." Trent rolled his eyes. "I told her before I put in sod at that apartment complex next door that she was going to have to take care of it for the first two weeks. She expected me to do it for free, but that's not part of the service."

Sam nodded encouragingly.

Trent continued. "I explained to her that she needed to water it twice a day, early in the morning and late in the evening, and for how long. At the time, I worked out of my home, but a day or two later, I was in this part of town. I could tell just driving by that she wasn't doing anything. I even had my assistant call and remind her. And then she had the gall to say it was my fault the grass died and to tell people all over town that my lawn care service couldn't be trusted."

"I know you said you didn't kill her. But as someone who used to own his own company, I can tell you that if someone did that to me, it would have made me mad," Sam said.

"It did make me mad at the time," Trent said. "And I may have told a few people who were trying to find an apartment that Patti Sue's complex was the last place they wanted to live."

Interesting. He had sought revenge, but, if I believed him, it had been more of a tit-for-tat retaliation, not an escalation to murder.

"That was all I did, a couple of weeks of mudslinging," Trent said. "Besides, this was a year and a half ago, not that long after her husband died and she took over running the apartments." He brushed a finger along one shiny leaf of a nearby hosta. "Oddly enough, losing that lawn care business may have been the best thing that ever happened to me."

"It was?" I stared at him, confused. This guy seemed almost too nice. After all, I'd practically accused him of murder. But for all I knew, it was an act.

"Yeah, a couple of months after my business tanked, my wife inherited money from her great-uncle when he passed away. If the lawn care business had been going well, we would have saved the money and continued with what we were doing, me taking care of people's yards, and her working as a secretary at the university. But because I was trying to figure out what to do with myself, it made us start talking about what we really wanted, and we decided to open this place together. Did you notice those terrariums when you walked in?"

"I did. They're adorable." So adorable I wouldn't mind taking one home with me.

"That's all my wife's doing. People come all the way from St. Louis to buy those things. And I have to say, dealing with all sorts of plants is a lot more rewarding than only dealing with grass. I love working with my wife, and I love all the cool products we're able to sell. So," he said with a half-smile, "I'm sort of glad that Patti Sue didn't water her sod."

"And you ended up putting your greenhouse right next to the apartments she owns?" I would think, after their history, Patti Sue would have been the last person Trent wanted for a business neighbor.

"Weird, I admit," he said. "But the spot was close to town, the price wasn't outrageous, and this central building was already here. Greenhouses go up fast."

Sam leaned his weight back on his heels and slid his hands into his back pockets. "People wouldn't use you for lawn care, but they'd buy their plants here?"

"Yeah," Trent said. "It was a gamble to open a business in a related field, but it was what my wife and I both wanted. We sell so much more than plants. I think those gift items helped us get established. Once they were in the door, people could see how healthy our plants were. And when you buy a plant at a greenhouse, there's no question that it's your responsibility to water it when you take it home."

"That makes sense." All the plants were lush and gorgeous. And I did believe that good could come out of a bad turn of events. "So, if you're not the killer, do you have any idea who it might be?"

Trent barked out a laugh. "That woman was so difficult, it could be anyone in town."

"With her business right next door, did you ever notice anything? Or overhear a comment from a customer in your shop?" Sam said.

"Sorry. I can't help you at all. I can understand how it's hurting things at the museum." Trent dipped his head toward me. "I wish you luck. If someone was at the high school on Saturday and they knew Patti Sue, I'd say there's a strong probability they didn't like her. There could be hundreds of suspects."

Well, not really. Not everyone had been in the hallway near the bathrooms at the time of the murder. I thanked him and headed back into the main shop with Sam. I gazed once more at the terrariums but backed away when I saw the price tags. With a sigh, I turned toward the door.

"He doesn't seem like a very likely suspect, does he?" Sam said as we climbed into his car.

"No, at first he seemed too nice to be true, but, despite the malice behind what Patti Sue did, she actually ended up helping him."

"I can even understand why they don't allow pets," Sam

said. "Can you imagine Bella wagging her tail near all those stained-glass ornaments? That wouldn't end well."

"No. But neither will this case if I can't figure out who the killer is." My shoulders slumped, and I sank down into the car seat.

Sam reluctantly dropped me off and hurried to the student organization meeting where he was speaking that evening. I went inside, told Bella what I'd learned so far, and hunted around in the freezer until I found some frozen enchiladas. Then I stood, watching the glass turntable spin inside the microwave and tapping one foot.

Somehow, somewhere, I needed to come up with a clue that would blow this case wide open.

Chapter Twelve

THE NEXT MORNING promised to be the hottest day yet
since I'd moved to Dogwood Springs.

Even though Bella and I were out for our walk before
eight, the air was already sticky. I cut things short, turning
around at Eleventh Street, and we slowly went back home. I
floated four ice cubes in her water bowl, took a cool shower,
and put on a loose, flowy dress for the day. I added earrings
and my great-great-grandmother's pearls and called it good.
Because the temperature was supposed to be over 100°F, I
drove to work. I spent the drive and a lot of the morning
thinking about Patti Sue's murder.

About eleven thirty, I made a quick trip home to let
Bella out. Once I returned to the museum, I dug into some
research about early ironworks in the area. The information
was so fascinating that for the first time all day, I was able to
completely forget about the murder. I continued reading,
nibbling away at a ham sandwich and some sour cream-

and-cheddar potato chips I'd brought. I was pulling out my dessert, four small shortbread cookies, when my phone dinged with a text.

Zeke Anderson
Remember how Jade told U she could never have killed Patti Sue cuz she was a vegetarian?

Yes.

Just saw her in the parking lot behind the Burger Barn. Eating a hamburger.

Maybe it was a veggie burger?

Zeke sent a laughing emoji with tears running down its face.

Never eaten at the Burger Barn, have U, Libby?

No.

The Burger Barn was on the edge of town, kind of out of the way, and frankly, pretty run-down. It struck me as the type of place where the tables might appear clean, but if you used the restroom, you'd wonder about health code violations in the kitchen.

Little dots appeared. Zeke seemed to be typing a longer message.

The menu only has 4 items. Fries, the Burger, the Big Burger, and the Heart Attack. That's a triple burger with 3 slices of cheese and 2 layers of bacon.

A tingle of excitement ran through my chest. I texted back.

Jade lied.

Looks like it to me.

And if she lied about being a vegetarian, what else did she lie about? I quickly typed in a reply.

This is a great clue, Zeke. I'll see if Cleo's free to go with me to talk to Jade again.

He sent a little hand waving goodbye, and my phone went silent.

I spun my chair and gazed out the window at the sun beating down on my car. Without even touching the glass, I could feel the heat seeping through. The temperature inside my car was probably 150°F, but I couldn't wait to climb in, drive over to the apartment complex, and continue the investigation.

Because this clue about Jade made a lot of sense.

Chip was definitely a jerk, but his motive for killing Patti Sue seemed weak. Gene saw the apartment complex as a barrier to the life he wanted, not something to kill for. Noreen acted guilty over even considering a practical joke. And although Patti Sue annoyed her, Edna seemed to have risen above the situation and proceeded through life with calm compassion.

But Jade …

Jade had worked with Patti Sue and endured emotional abuse day after day after day. I could easily imagine that it could have built up to be more than she could stand. And she'd created quite the lie, telling us she was a vegetarian and didn't even kill bugs. I could totally see her as the murderer.

Suddenly, though, Trent's question about my safety niggled at the back of my brain. Was I being foolish, confronting a woman for the second time if I thought she was a killer? One interaction might be believable as a somewhat casual conversation, but twice?

Not likely.

Maybe I should call Detective Harper and tell him what I'd learned. After all, Jade had no alibi, a fairly strong motive, and had argued with Patti Sue right before the murder.

I sat at my desk, tipping a pen back and forth between my hands, trying to decide. Part of me, I had to admit, liked being the person who solved a mystery. And I had seen on more than one occasion how Detective Harper tended to get fixated on one suspect and ignore other possibilities. On the other hand, if I told him my suspicions about Jade, I might be able to convince him to follow up on them.

I set down my pen, grabbed the receiver from the phone on my desk, and called the local police station.

Five minutes later, after a long time on hold and a brief

conversation, I hung up. Detective Harper was in St. Louis at a mandatory training seminar until tomorrow.

The decision had been taken out of my hands.

I couldn't in good conscience ignore what I'd learned for twenty-four hours. I knew, from what Sue Ann, the police dispatcher, had told Cleo, that Detective Harper was the best of the lot as far as interviewing suspects in the Dogwood Springs Police Department. And I wouldn't confront Jade alone.

I dug my phone out of my purse and texted Cleo. Was she available to go with me to talk to Jade again?

A minute later Cleo replied. She had a small window between clients shortly after I got off work. If I promised to drive through somewhere on our way back so she could get a sandwich, she'd go with me.

Perfect. The apartment complex office was open until six. If we hurried, we could be there in time to talk to Jade.

At five, I drove home to let Bella out. I hadn't been planning to bring her along, but she seemed so starved for attention that I made a deal with her. I wouldn't take time to feed her, but I'd bring along two doggy treats. She could ride along with Cleo and me, and I'd feed her as soon as we were home.

She sniffed at the cabinet where I stored her kibble, but, when I jingled her leash and opened the back door, she trotted out with me. There was a slight delay when I had to explain that Cleo would be sitting in the front seat. But once Bella was settled in the back, I delivered the treats, texted Cleo that I was on my way, and headed toward her salon.

Although Cleo sent a thumbs-up reply, she didn't immediately appear when I pulled into the parking lot behind her salon.

I was about to text her again when the back screen door banged open, and Cleo dashed out.

"I'm so sorry. Last minute crisis." She climbed in, strapped on her seatbelt, and pulled her T-shirt out from her collarbone a few times as if trying to cool off. "Could it get any hotter?"

I pulled out onto the street and, as we drove by the bank, pointed at the thermometer displaying a temperature of 103°F. "Thanks for going with me today, in spite of the heat."

"If Jade's the killer, she needs to be stopped," Cleo said. "You get her to confess, and, if need be, I'll disable her with one of the self-defense moves I learned when I lived in New York."

Bella gave a loud woof as if also volunteering to help.

As we drove, I told Cleo more about the hidden letter and how Sam thought his parents would be interested to hear about the new historical mystery we'd found.

"They're here on Saturday, right?" Cleo glanced over at me.

"Uh-huh. The day after tomorrow."

"Don't sound so worried. They're going to love you."

I gave her a wry smile. "I don't know. If my son was as

wealthy as Sam, I'd be afraid every woman he saw was only out for his money."

Cleo let out a snort. "Once they meet you and see what a genuine person you are, they'll know you like Sam for who he is, not for his money."

I wasn't convinced.

"Trust me. You and Sam belong together." She let out a sigh. "It always amazes me when people doubt the obvious."

I stared straight ahead. If I looked Cleo in the eye, I'd have a hard time not letting it show that I thought she was missing some serious irony. After all, Bryce had broken up with his fiancée before she was murdered. Their relationship had been over. And I'd seen the way Bryce looked at Cleo.

But she seemed uncomfortable even waving to him on the street.

I thought back on how, at first, after his fiancée had been murdered, Bryce and Cleo had spent time together. Not actual dates, but coffee every couple of weeks. She'd even stopped seeing that pediatrician she had been dating. And then, nothing. I ran a hand over my jaw.

Could something have happened? A kiss perhaps? Or had she run into Darcy's parents and felt that if she dated Bryce, it might be painful for them because it hadn't been that long since Darcy died?

I sat up taller. Oh, I could totally see that. And now Cleo was avoiding him.

Of course, maybe I had it all wrong. But I was going to watch for more clues.

I pulled into the parking lot of Hartley Road Apartments.

The small parking area in front of the office held only one car, which I assumed was Jade's. I parked beside it in the shade of a big oak. I certainly wasn't leaving Bella in the car, but if she wasn't allowed in the apartment office, I'd tie her to the tree. And she didn't need to walk on pavement so hot that it was practically melting.

The three of us climbed out, I clipped on Bella's leash, and we headed toward the door.

"Knock, knock," I called as I opened the door. "Hot enough for you, Jade?"

"Oh, no!" Cleo gasped and raced to the side of the desk, where Jade lay awkwardly on the carpet.

Bella surged forward, barking.

I edged her aside and moved closer to Jade. "Maybe she had some sort of heart trouble." I took her shoulders, and Cleo took her legs, and we laid her out flat on the floor.

"Or a seizure or something," Cleo said.

But when I looked down, a chill shot through me.

Jade hadn't passed out from a medical condition. A deep, red line cut into her throat, running all around her neck.

Jade, like Patti Sue, had been strangled.

My stomach tightened into a knot. I pressed my fingertips against the side of Jade's neck, then shook my head at Cleo.

She stood and backed away from the body, scanning the room. "How many ways are there into this building?"

"Probably two." Although the office building was only one story, not two like the rest of the complex, the office appeared to be a regular apartment unit. The others we had driven past had a back door that opened onto a small patio.

So, presumably, even if the killer had been in the office a few minutes ago, they could have slipped out the back door.

Or into a closet.

Cleo gestured toward the door we'd come in. "Let's wait for the police in the car."

"Good idea." I tugged on Bella's leash, and the three of us hurried outside, got back in my car, and locked the doors.

Cleo was already dialing her phone and soon began speaking with the 911 operator. "They're on their way," she said to me.

I didn't want to stick around, but it didn't feel right to drive away, so I kept scanning the area. I would think that after the murderer killed Jade, they would have left as fast as possible, but maybe logic wasn't part of the equation.

Bella leaned her head over my shoulder, panting.

Oddly enough, I felt cold. Shock, perhaps. But Bella was clearly hot, so I turned on the car and started the air conditioning.

I reached into the pocket behind Cleo's seat and pulled out two water bottles. I offered one to her, but she declined. I put it back and set the other bottle in the console to remind me to give some to Bella as soon as we felt safe to get out of the car.

I looked over at Cleo, who was still on the phone. "I really thought Jade was the killer."

"Me too," she mouthed.

But we'd both been wrong. She'd simply been a friendly woman who worked for a difficult boss. And now, she was dead.

Eventually, a siren wailed in the distance, and then grew closer.

Soon Officers Tate and Davis arrived, along with two younger officers that I didn't know. Officer Tate stayed with us, and the others went inside to investigate. A few minutes later, they radioed back to say that the perpetrator was nowhere to be seen.

I got out, took Bella under the big oak, and gave her some water in a travel bowl I kept in the car. While she drank, traffic hummed on Hartley Road, and birds twittered in nearby trees as if it were a normal day. As if no one had been murdered a few yards from where I stood.

As soon as Bella had drunk her fill, I called her over, and we got back in the car.

I sat next to Cleo, wrapped my arms around myself, and tucked my shaking hands under my arms. Cleo was pale, and she'd sunk back into her seat, twisting a ring on one finger.

Bella stuck her head between the two front seats and nuzzled her head against my arm, then against Cleo's. I wouldn't be surprised if she could sense the tension rolling off us.

After about ten minutes, Officer Tate tapped on my window.

Cleo and I got out, and he introduced us to Detective Sanders, who was handling the case until Detective Harper returned to town.

The detective questioned both Cleo and me, but his questions felt routine, and he treated me as I would imagine he'd treat anyone who'd just found a dead body. He didn't act surprised or annoyed that I'd been at the scene of the crime. He didn't say a word about keeping my nose out of the case. And to be honest, he didn't seem that on the ball.

Eventually, Cleo and I were allowed to leave, and I turned my car onto Hartley Road. "Do you still want me to drive through someplace so you can get dinner?"

"No, thanks," she said. "I don't want to eat. It's bad enough that I have to go back to work."

I dipped my head in sympathy. "Detective Sanders is never going to find the killer, is he?"

She shook her head.

"But if Valerie has an alibi for when Jade was killed, then Detective Harper should stop suspecting her."

"That would be good," Cleo said. "We need to find out what she was doing today."

"On the other hand, Jade was our top suspect. With her dead, we don't have a clue who the killer is. And it's even more important now that we figure this out."

"This killer needs to be stopped," Cleo agreed.

"When are you done at the salon tonight?"

"Seven thirty."

"Can you text our friends to see if they can meet us at the Dogwood Café at eight? Would that work for you?"

"Sounds good." Cleo began typing into her phone. "And I'll ask Alice to see if Valerie has an alibi for when Jade was killed."

"Thanks. We've got to solve this before someone else gets murdered." I turned toward Cleo's salon, and I tried to keep my mind on my driving.

But my thoughts kept drifting back to the image of Jade's lifeless body.

Chapter Thirteen

ONCE WE GOT BACK to Elm Street, I fed Bella and took a long shower. Then I put on shorts and a T-shirt and collapsed onto my couch.

The minute I sat down, Bella carried over her favorite toy, a well-chewed stuffed chicken, and dropped it at my feet.

I ran a hand over the silky fur on the top of her head and sat there, silent, as she gazed up at me with her big brown eyes shining, her mouth open in a wide doggy grin.

Eventually, the horror of the murder receded slightly, and I realized it was almost time to leave. I slipped on my tennis shoes, stepped into the entryway, and called up the stairs to Cleo, who I'd heard come in a few minutes ago.

She came down a moment later and stuck her head in my apartment. "I'm ready."

There was a *clunk* from my kitchen, and Bella appeared

with the handle of her leash in her mouth, the end trailing behind her. Apparently, she'd picked up on the plan.

I clipped the leash onto her collar, and we headed out toward downtown.

The temperature had cooled considerably, back into normal Missouri summer heat, and we saw three kids riding their bikes as well as a boy practicing soccer kicks into a net.

Bella stopped to get her ears scratched by the boy practicing soccer, but Cleo was subdued, only brightening as we neared the café.

The sun had dropped below the rooftops of the buildings across the street, and even from half a block away, I could tell the outdoor seating was packed with people laughing and chatting.

It almost felt wrong to be in a place where people were so happy after Jade's death. And yet, I longed to be on the patio, surrounded by people untouched by murder. I needed that normalcy, needed that connection to the supportive community that—despite these recent murders—was the essence of Dogwood Springs. I started walking faster.

A couple of minutes later, Cleo waved to Alice, who was already sitting at our favorite table in the back corner of the patio.

Cleo led the way through the seating area, weaving her way through the tables, and Bella and I followed. Bella, of course, stopped at almost every table to say hello to other diners.

Soon Sam and Zeke arrived, and Sam pulled me into a tight hug and pressed a kiss into my hair.

Alice embraced Cleo and patted my arm. "Oh, you poor dears. Are you all right?"

"Yeah," Cleo said. "But I was shaken up for a while and didn't want dinner."

I said the same.

"It would do you both good to eat something now," Sam said. "How about toast?"

"Maybe a bite or two." I sat, and soon we were all settled around the table.

The server must have heard Sam because she appeared at our table and took our drink and food orders. She returned almost instantly with my iced tea, Cleo's Diet Dr. Pepper, Alice's iced coffee, and Sam and Zeke's cherry sodas.

I pulled a water bottle and collapsible bowl out of my oversized purse and gave Bella water and a dog biscuit.

"I still can't believe Jade was murdered," Cleo said once the server had walked away.

"I was sure after the way she lied about being a vegetarian that she was the killer." Zeke unwrapped his straw, wadded up the wrapper, and tossed it at Sam.

Sam caught it in mid-air, and Cleo gave Zeke an "at least pretend you have good manners" glare.

Sam slid his soda cup in front of him and wrapped both hands around it. "Maybe Jade realized that she looked like a likely suspect because of how she'd been fighting with Patti

Sue, and she lied because she was afraid people might think she was the killer."

"You may be right," I said. "Whatever the reason for her lie, it had us going down completely the wrong path. We need to rethink everything." I looked at Alice. "Did you have a chance to talk to Valerie?"

Alice let out a sigh. "I did. She says she was home alone all day."

"So no alibi. That's a shame." I ran my hands down my thighs. "We're just going to have to keep trying."

Alice nodded. "We have five other people left who had access to the hallway at the time of Patti Sue's murder." She raised a hand and counted on her fingers as she named them. "Trent, Noreen, Chip, Edna, and Gene. And whoever the murderer is, they needed a reason to kill both Patti Sue and Jade."

"It could be," I said, "that Jade saw the killer in the hallway near the time of the murder but didn't put it together right away. And later she did."

"That seems reasonable," Cleo said. "And somehow the killer figured that out."

"We also need to think about the fact that this person has now killed more than once," Sam said. "They're very dangerous. And what if they think other people might have seen them as well? They could kill again."

The five of us exchanged worried glances.

"Is there some angle we've missed?" I said.

Sam stared off into the distance. Alice stirred her iced

coffee. Cleo silently tapped a finger on the table, and Zeke scratched his chin.

At the back of my mind, an idea hovered just out of my grasp. I closed my eyes and tried to focus.

"Oh," I sat up. "Let me check something." I pulled out my phone and scrolled through the reviews of Hartley Road Apartments.

The server arrived, and Zeke leaned back in his chair as she slid a plate of nachos in front of him. We waited while she gave Sam a slice of apple pie, Alice a fruit cup, Cleo a bowl of vanilla pudding, and me an order of buttered wheat toast. I set my phone to the side of my plate, kept scrolling, and slowly ate my toast.

For a while, the only sounds at our table were the scraping of silverware against dishes and the clink of ice in plastic cups.

From the reviews I read on my phone, it was clear that people weren't happy with how Patti Sue had run Hartley Road Apartments. Several reviewers voiced the same opinion Jade had, that the place had been much better when Patti Sue's husband was in charge. But most of the negative reviews were from people who had moved out and were offering a warning to others. I couldn't see them also feeling the need to kill Patti Sue. Maybe this was a waste of time and—

Hold on. I reread one of the reviews, then stared at the name of the person who posted it. "Listen to this. 'I lived at Hartley Road Apartments for three years,'" I quoted. "'Even though my rent was paid, I was wrongfully evicted due to circumstances beyond my control. The current manager is heartless. Do yourself a favor and don't even consider renting from her.'"

"If Patti Sue evicted someone, I could certainly see them being upset," Alice said. "It would be very traumatic, especially if they thought it was completely unfair."

"The reviewer is named 'Ladybug N,'" I added quickly.

"I'm not surprised at the comment, given how horrid Patti Sue was to people," Cleo said. "But it seems unlikely that that particular unhappy renter is one of the people who had access to the hallway to murder Patti Sue."

"It does seem unlikely," I admitted. "Until I tell you that when I ran into Noreen downtown yesterday, she was wearing ladybug earrings."

Cleo's eyes widened.

"Man, that's an excellent clue, Libby." Sam leaned back in his chair.

"Thanks. But how can we know that Noreen lived at Hartley Road Apartments and was evicted?"

Alice turned to Cleo. "One of us should have a friend who works at the hospital who would know, don't you think?"

"Definitely. I'll just need to make a few calls," Cleo said.

"Excellent." I sat up taller. Even though the case had gotten harder, even though I might not go to sleep for hours as I kept seeing Jade's dead body in my mind's eye, I wasn't giving up. "Depending on how traumatic it was, that eviction might well have been a motive for Noreen to murder Patti Sue."

Chapter Fourteen

I'D JUST PUT a few daisies I'd picked from my backyard into the three little vases on my desk the next morning when thunder rumbled, and rain began to pour down.

And I'd left my car windows cracked.

I raced outside, but it was too late. The cloth seats were already damp. I closed the windows, dried the seats off as best I could, and trudged back to my office, completely drenched.

I dried off with some paper towels from the bathroom and sat down at my desk. A moment later, Imani knocked, walked in, and sank into the chair across from me. I told her about my car windows.

"But we've got bigger problems what with Jade dead, don't we?" Imani gave a dramatic sigh.

"I was about to get you and Rodney together to tell you." I pulled a sweater from my desk drawer. "But you already heard."

"Oh, you know Dogwood Springs. Last night at the Community Center, they had a volleyball tournament, and the murders were all people could talk about." Imani pinched up her face and raised the pitch of her voice as if impersonating someone else. "'What's going on with the museum these days? They tried to host that historic fashion show, and two of the models have been killed. I don't know about you, but I'm more interested in self-preservation than I am in history.'"

My shoulders sank. "People were saying that?"

"It was all I heard. At first, I was ready to step in and tell people that the museum wasn't responsible. But Dale reminded me that until the killer is caught, it isn't going to matter what we say. If people don't have anyone else to blame, they'll blame the museum."

Sadly, her husband was right. Outside, a clap of thunder boomed.

"Eventually, I got so frustrated that we went home early," Imani said with disgust. "And we'd specially arranged for my mom to watch the baby and everything."

Rodney stuck his head in the door. His gray eyes, which usually shone with good humor, were tense. "Are you all talking about the second murder?"

We nodded.

"I'm sorry you found the body, Libby," he said. "That had to be shocking. And it certainly wasn't what the museum needed."

Imani leaned in toward me. "Have you made any progress in figuring out the killer? I mean, it's the police department's responsibility, but in the past ..." She let the question drift off.

I knew what she meant. In the past, when the museum had been affected by crime, I'd played a key role in bringing the perpetrator to justice. Although my hunch about Noreen might be a valuable clue, I didn't want to get Imani's hopes up. "Nothing yet," I said. "But I'm trying."

"Well." Imani stood. "I imagine that today I'll be able to get a lot of planning done for programming for school visits this fall. I don't expect we'll have very many visitors."

"You're right," Rodney said. "The place will be empty. But we can use that to our advantage." The two of them wandered into the hall, discussing a display that Rodney was setting up.

I crossed my fingers, hoped that my hunch about Noreen would turn out to be useful, and tried to focus on my work.

I opened my word processing program to draft an e-mail to our major donors regarding the current situation. Unfortunately, it wasn't a very easy e-mail to write. Ten minutes later, I was still struggling with the first paragraph when footsteps came down the hall toward my office.

"Ta-da!" Cleo shouted as she burst in, flipped back the hood of her rain slicker, and spread her hands wide. "Rodney let me in the back door, and I've got the whole scoop on Noreen."

A tingle of excitement shot through me, and I scooted my chair forward. "What did you find out?"

Cleo quickly sat down. "Last year about this time,

Noreen was renting from Patti Sue when her mother, who lived in Kansas City, died suddenly, and Noreen had to take in her dog, this cute little white Westie. According to my mom's friend at the hospital, the dog was very well-behaved and hardly ever barked. But the apartment complex doesn't allow pets."

"Uh-oh."

"Noreen went to Patti Sue and explained the situation. She said she was looking for a new place to live, and that at the very most, she might be in the apartment three more weeks."

"That seems reasonable," I said. "I mean, there wasn't anything else she could do when her mom died."

"Patti Sue wasn't in any way reasonable. And she showed absolutely no compassion for Noreen. She told her she and the dog had to be out the next day."

My mouth dropped open. "That's terrible."

"I know. It's also against the law. Patti Sue should have given her ten days to comply with the lease or move out. But at the time, Noreen was so upset about her mom that she didn't have the energy to fight it. She was in shock— simply reacting, not thinking."

"What did she do?"

"She went to a hotel that allowed pets, scrambled to find a new place, and moved over the weekend. Later, though, when her life calmed down, she thought back on how Patti Sue had treated her, and she was furious."

"So that, combined with the additional insult of how

Patti Sue insisted that she wear the lemon-yellow suit, might have pushed Noreen over the edge."

"Exactly," Cleo said.

"I think we need to go have another chat with Noreen."

"I'm way ahead of you. Every Friday, Noreen has lunch at the Chinese place near the hospital, and I had a client cancel a perm appointment at eleven thirty, so if you can get away from the museum ..."

I pulled up the calendar on my computer to be sure. It was wide open. "I sure can!"

"Great. I'll pick you up. I've got to run though. I've got a cut and color starting in—" Cleo checked her phone and let out a yelp. "Two minutes."

She dashed out the door, and I returned to my e-mail with more hope. Maybe we'd figure out this murder after all.

Two hours later, I struggled to keep the wind from turning my umbrella inside out as I climbed into Cleo's Jeep in the museum parking lot. We drove by our house so I could let Bella out, and I got even wetter. But by the time we passed the hospital on Hartley Road, I'd managed to rearrange my hair into some semblance of order.

The Chinese place near the hospital, Wok and Roll, was new to me. Normally, when Sam and I went out, we had Mexican food because he knew I loved it. When we opted for Chinese, we went to a place closer to the university. But Wok and Roll was clearly popular. The parking lot was packed, and it was only by sheer luck that Cleo found a spot near the door.

We raised our umbrellas and dashed inside.

The restaurant had bare bones decorating—Formica tables, worn booths, and metal chairs—but it was spotless. I caught a whiff of crab Rangoon as it passed on a server's tray, and my mouth began watering. Traditional Asian music played softly in the background, and a TV high in one corner of the room aired a soccer game.

Sure enough, Noreen was there, sitting alone at a booth. She wore lavender scrubs and a different, larger pair of ladybug earrings.

"Perfect. Whoever she's meeting isn't here yet," I said.

Cleo and I squeezed between two large parties that had awkwardly pushed tables together, and we hurried over to stand by Noreen's table. We said hello, and she looked at us expectantly.

"You weren't exactly honest with us before, Noreen," Cleo said.

"Yeah," I added. "We heard about how horrible Patti Sue was when your mother passed away, evicting you when you had taken in her dog."

Noreen's face hardened. "I didn't think it was any of your business," she spat out. "It was more than a year ago, and it's irrelevant now."

"Really?" I leaned in and kept my voice down. "What if

the way Patti Sue was so selfish about wearing the 1940s suit made you angrier and pushed you over the edge?"

Noreen's forehead pinched together, and she tilted her head to one side. "Libby, I understand that historic fashion show mattered a lot to you, but to the rest of the world ... not so much."

Okay, she might have a point.

"But Patti Sue was so heartless about the dog," Cleo said, "especially considering you had just lost your mom."

"She was." Noreen crossed her arms over her chest. "But I'm not the murderer, and I can prove it. I heard how Jade was killed yesterday afternoon at Hartley Road Apartments. I worked a twelve-hour shift yesterday, seven to seven. I couldn't have gone to the apartments in the afternoon."

Oh, a solid alibi. "That makes sense."

"Believe me, I'm not the killer," Noreen said firmly.

I did think the murders were related. "I'm sorry we bothered you. The killer needs to be stopped, though, so if you think of anything ..."

She narrowed her eyes, stared off to one side, and drew her lips up tight.

A tingle of hope ran through me. "Do you have something that might help us?"

After a second, she let out a sigh. "The last thing I want to do is send you two off to wrongly accuse someone else, but I did hear something that made me wonder." She angled her head at the booth across from her.

Cleo and I slid into it. "What did you hear?" I asked.

Noreen hesitated as if she might reconsider, then shrugged. "Someone told me that Edna Hughes's son has a drug problem. I'm sure Edna would be mortified if that was all over town. If Patti Sue found out and told Edna that she knew..."

"I could see that happening." Cleo nodded so enthusiastically that her bangs moved. "Patti Sue loved to lord it over someone when she knew dirt on them."

"Don't you know it," Noreen said. "What if Edna wanted to stop Patti Sue from telling all of Dogwood Springs ..." She spread her hands wide. "Well, it would give her a strong motive for killing Patti Sue."

Noreen gave Cleo and me a pointed stare. "A strong, obvious motive. One that isn't a year old."

I shifted uncomfortably in my seat.

In a flash, Noreen's face brightened, and she waved to someone behind us. "My friend just walked in." Her smile disappeared as she looked back at Cleo and me. "I appreciate what you're trying to do, but I'd like you to leave. I want to enjoy lunch with my friend, not think about murder or the time when my mom died."

Cleo and I slid out of the booth and, despite the best efforts of the server to stop us and offer us a table, hurried out of the restaurant and back into the rain.

"Well," Cleo said once we were back in her Jeep. "What do you think?"

"I think I'll have to do some sweet-talking if I expect Noreen to do any more volunteer work at the museum."

Cleo dipped her head in agreement.

"And I think I need to have another talk with Edna." I

fastened my seat belt. "If Patti Sue not only lied about Edna's husband but was also telling secrets about her son, it may have pushed her over the edge."

"I think you're right." Cleo put her Jeep in gear. "Maybe she could handle Patti Sue's gossip when she knew it wasn't true, but when it was something she couldn't deny, it was too much."

Chapter Fifteen

BACK IN MY office at the museum, I took my turkey sandwich out of my thermal lunch box and unwrapped it. After the amazing smells of Wok and Roll and the thought of my favorites—crab Rangoon and Moo Shu pork—the lunch I brought from home seemed like a consolation prize. I promised myself some good Chinese food soon and settled down, eating my sandwich while reviewing the dismal recent attendance numbers for the museum.

Half an hour later, I took a break and sent a quick text to Alice, and we came up with a plan to talk to Edna again. Alice was supposed to play cards that evening and didn't have long, but we both remembered Edna's comments about Bella and thought we should bring her with us.

Finally, we decided that since my car seats were probably still wet, Alice would pick me up, we'd drive by my house, and I'd run in to get Bella. I was a little worried about Bella's toenails damaging the upholstery in Alice's

SUV and the mud she might track in, but Alice pointed out that she had plastic floor mats. And she assured me she had a blanket she could toss over the back seat. Apparently, as a grandmother of twin little boys, she traveled prepared.

As I was leaving, I noticed that Rodney was still working, updating our display on the history of railroads in the area before he went out of town for a wedding over the weekend.

I wished him a good time and headed out into the rain.

When I dashed into my apartment, I told Bella that dinner would be slightly delayed because she was going to see an old friend. She seemed to understand because she trotted to the kitchen door without even a glimpse at the cabinet with the dog food. I kept us as dry as possible and made sure Bella stayed on the sidewalk and gravel rather than the muddy grass as we walked to Alice's car.

Once Bella and I were settled, Alice turned onto Elm Street, and right after five thirty, we pulled into Edna's driveway. The rain had eased up a bit, but the sky was still a dark, bluish gray.

"I hope she's home," I said. "I was hesitant to tell her we were coming to talk to her again." I undid my seatbelt and grabbed my purse from behind the passenger seat. "I guess we take our chances."

"The curtains just moved." Alice angled her head toward the house. "She's home."

We climbed out, and I hooked Bella's leash onto her collar. "Time to be your most charming self," I told her.

"Stay right beside me, on the driveway so your paws stay clean."

We'd barely taken three steps when the front door opened. "You brought Bella to visit?" Edna's eyes lit up as she bent down, and her voice filled with delight. "Hello, girl!"

Bella surged to meet her on the covered porch. "Don't get too excited, Bella." I didn't want her jumping up on Edna, especially not with wet paws.

Edna bent down and petted Bella. "Hold on." She dashed inside, returned with a towel, and wiped her off.

Bella's tail swished back and forth, and she quivered with excitement as Edna scratched her ears. "It's been a while, hasn't it, Bella? I haven't gotten to talk to you since your former owner passed away." She glanced up at me, eyes shining. "But I'm glad you found a new home."

Bella nuzzled her head against Edna's leg, and Edna invited us in. We left our umbrellas on the porch and wiped our feet, then followed her to the living room where the same slowly ticking grandfather clock greeted us.

Edna gestured toward the couch. "Have a seat. Did you just come over to let Bella visit, or was there something else you needed, Libby?"

Alice and I sat down. Edna was being so nice, and Bella seemed to like her so much that my stomach tightened even considering her as a murderer. But I needed to know. "I heard something that gave me pause. It involves your son."

The joy disappeared from Edna's eyes, and she pulled her arms close to her body.

I continued. "The person I was speaking with mentioned that your son was going through a difficult patch and thought Patti Sue might have learned about it."

"Libby and I realize addiction is a disease," Alice said softly. "We also understand that you might be uncomfortable with everyone in town hearing about your son's issues."

"It was even suggested," I added, "that you might have killed Patti Sue to keep your secret quiet. And then killed Jade to cover it up."

Edna let out a long sigh, and her shoulders sank. For a moment I wasn't sure if she was going to say anything.

"Part of what you heard is true," she said at last, her voice shaking. "My son worked for a construction company and got injured on the job. I blame that doctor for even starting him on those painkillers, but pointing fingers doesn't solve the problem." She gave an uneven smile. "And Patti Sue had heard all about it. I don't know who felt the need to tell her."

Edna tipped her head toward Alice. "You can understand, can't you, Alice? How ugly Patti Sue could be? The woman had no heart at all."

"I can," Alice said gently.

Edna turned to gaze behind her at a framed photograph of a man who had to be her son, a pretty blond woman, and a little girl with blond curls.

My stomach tightened even more. Normally, I was only focused on justice, but right now, I didn't want to hear what she said next. I didn't want her to be the murderer. I didn't want to be the reason she ended up in jail.

I wished I'd never come to her door.

Edna turned back to face us. "I can't say that I'm sorry she's dead, but I didn't kill her, I swear."

My stomach eased a little. Maybe she wasn't the killer.

Edna rested her hands on her thighs and leaned forward. "Libby, I've been a rule follower all my life. As a little kid, if I ever got pulled along by a crowd to do something we shouldn't, I was the one who got caught. Sometimes the only one."

I sat back, surprised. I'd thought I was the only person like that.

"I think," Edna continued, "I internalized the message that other people could break rules and get away with it and not even feel guilty, but that wasn't the path for me. And murder?" She sniffed. "If I committed murder, I know I'd get arrested. How would that help my son? Having to find me a lawyer and visit me in jail? None of that would help get him off drugs."

"True," Alice said softly.

"So yes, we've got a real problem in our family." Edna stopped and pressed her eyes tightly shut as if forcing back tears. "And thanks to Patti Sue's gossiping, apparently, it's all over town. But he's started a treatment plan, and his wife and I will both do anything we can to help him. We hope, with our support, he can kick this habit. And with luck, people will forget about it in time."

"I think they will," Alice said. "And even if they don't, they'll be more understanding than you think. Sometimes our own issues get magnified in our perception, but everybody's family has problems, even if we aren't aware of them."

Edna nodded and blinked.

Bella, who had been sitting quietly by Edna's side, stood and rested her head on Edna's leg. Edna bent down, running her fingers over Bella's fur, and her shoulders rose and fell.

I waited a moment, giving her time to pull herself together. "Thanks for talking with us. We didn't want to wait and risk interrupting your dinner, but I think Bella knows it's past time for her to eat."

Edna gave a weak chuckle. "Oh, I remember Don telling me about Bella. 'Smartest dog in town,' he always claimed. She probably does know it's past her dinner time."

After letting Edna and Bella spend a few more moments together, Alice and I walked to the door, and Bella reluctantly joined us.

"Good luck finding the killer," Edna said. "Wish I could help."

We thanked her again for her time and made our way back through the rain to Alice's car.

I settled Bella in the back seat and climbed in. "Bella really likes Edna. It may be foolish, but I'm learning to trust her judgment of people. But Edna doesn't have an alibi like Noreen does. I don't think we can completely rule her out as a suspect."

"And protecting a child is an incredibly strong motive," Alice said. "Some people will do almost anything for their family, even kill."

The sky grew darker as Alice drove back to the museum to drop Bella and me off at my car. Clouds hung low and black and heavy, and the rain, which had tapered for a while, shifted to a steady downpour.

When Alice turned into the gravel parking lot behind the museum, her lights glinted off my car, sitting there all alone. I started to bend down to pick up my umbrella and then peered back out. Something looked wrong but—

"One of my—no, *both* of my back tires are flat." I pointed.

"Libby, nobody gets two flat tires at once." Alice pulled her car alongside mine.

I looked more closely, and a shiver ran down my spine. "It's not just two tires. I think all four of them are flat. Someone ... someone slashed them." My stomach tensed, and I shrank back into the upholstered seat.

"Good grief." Alice ran a hand over her chest. "I can't leave you here alone." She pulled out her phone. "You call the police, and I'm canceling on my cards group tonight. They can play without me."

"Thank you." I peered out into the darkness, but I didn't see anyone.

On the other hand, the killer knew who I was, knew I'd

been investigating the murder, and knew where I worked. I didn't have any assurance that they weren't hiding behind a tree or the edge of the museum, watching and waiting for me to climb out of Alice's SUV.

I drew in a shaky breath and called the police.

Two officers arrived quickly, followed by Detective Harper.

The detective wasn't very happy to learn what had happened. It was obvious, he said, that I'd been ignoring his warning to stay out of the investigation.

He told the officers to collect any evidence that might have survived the rain and suggested we go inside so he could get my statement. I urged Alice to go on to her card game, but she refused. She said she'd wait for me in her car, that the officers would be right there close by, and so there was no need for me to worry.

I opened the museum and led the way into the conference room. Detective Harper sat across from me at the long table, patted Bella, and then gave me an unmistakable disapproving-Dad stare. "This is a strong message from the killer, Libby. They know you're trying to find them. You need to leave this alone. You're too nosy for your own good, but I don't want anything to happen to you."

I didn't either. Had I been foolish to get involved?

In my mind, finding the killer was, in a way, helping the museum. But how much was I helping if someone's car could be vandalized in the museum parking lot? And for someone who'd already killed twice, the distance between stabbing my tires and stabbing me didn't seem like that much of a leap. Should I just give up?

Possibly, but ... "I still don't believe Valerie is the killer."

"Okay." The detective flipped the page of his notebook and sat with his pen at the ready. "Who do you think it is?"

I ran through the five suspects in my mind.

Noreen had an alibi for Jade's murder, and I really believed the two crimes were connected.

Edna didn't have an alibi, but she didn't strike me as a killer. When she said she thought that if she committed a crime, she'd end up in jail, I believed her.

Gene didn't even want the apartment complex, and he seemed so beaten down by grief that I couldn't picture him having the energy to kill two people.

Chip didn't have a strong motive.

And in a weird way, Trent actually felt grateful to Patti Sue.

"Well?" the detective narrowed his eyes at me.

My stomach sank. "I don't know."

"Then, for your own safety, you need to leave the investigation to the professionals." He flipped his notebook shut. "Trust me, Libby. I haven't figured it out yet, but I am working on this case. I will get to the bottom of this. I know you've solved murder cases in the past, and I know you've come away unharmed. But you can't count on luck to keep you safe if you put yourself in danger."

I gave a weak nod. I wanted justice to be served, but deep down I knew he was right. And it wasn't as if I had any more leads.

I arranged for my car to be towed to a local garage once the police were finished, and Alice drove Bella and me home.

I'd called Cleo, and she stood on the front porch with what looked like every light turned on in the place.

I waved to Alice and tried to keep Bella dry as we hurried toward the house. Despite my efforts, by the time we reached the porch, I was soaked and chilled to the bone.

"You poor thing." Cleo hugged me and wiped off Bella's muddy paws with an old towel. "I let myself into your apartment, and I checked it out. It's all safe."

"Thank you." My voice cracked with emotion. What would I do without Alice, who had canceled her plans to protect me, and Cleo, who was making sure I was safe?

I went in, filled Bella's food bowl, and took a long, hot shower. Sam called, said he'd talked to Alice, and offered to come over and sleep on my couch. I assured him that I was fine, let Bella out for a quick trip to the backyard, and collapsed into bed.

Then I just lay there, awake.

From the way the detective talked, he was no closer to figuring out the killer than I was. And the killer knew where I worked. In a town this size, they could easily learn where I lived.

Even if I did stop trying to find them, would they know I'd stopped?

Would they think I no longer posed a risk to them?

Probably not.

Which meant this murder investigation wasn't about justice anymore. At least, not entirely.

It was also about my own safety.

Chapter Sixteen

IN THE LIGHT of day the next morning, my fears receded. And my determination to find the killer grew, especially when the tire place called to say my car would be ready to pick up at noon and told me what four new tires would cost.

Two people dead, and I was out more than eight hundred dollars. Oh, I knew the money wasn't as important as the loss of life, but it irked me. And, clearly, the situation now was personal.

As soon as I hung up, the caller ID showed an incoming call from Sam.

A cowardly hope sprung up in my chest. Was he calling to say his parents had changed their plans and weren't coming to town, and we would be dining without them tonight?

No, it turned out the dinner was still on. Sam simply wanted to see how I was.

"I'm doing okay." I explained that my car would be repaired by noon and that I was more determined than ever to figure out who the perpetrator was.

"I don't know how we figure out who slashed your tires," Sam said. "But I'd be happy to take you to get your car. If you'd like, we could also do a little more investigating into that old letter we found."

"You've got a lead?" I asked.

"Adrienne, my interior designer, should be back in town today. We could stop by and ask her where she bought the bookcase."

"Oh, I'd love a ride to get my car and a chance to do a little historical sleuthing."

"Do you think Bella would like to come along?" Sam asked. "Adrienne loves dogs. I'm sure Bella would be welcome."

I gave Bella a scratch behind the ears. "What do you say, girl? Would you like to spend some time with Sam?"

She replied with a happy woof that I took to be an affirmative response.

"How about I pick you up at ten thirty?" Sam said.

"Sounds perfect."

At ten thirty on the dot, Sam's car pulled into my driveway. I ducked into the kitchen to get Bella's leash, and by the time I returned to the living room, I spotted him through the windows, walking toward the front door of the house.

I stepped into the entryway and preempted his knock by opening the door to the porch.

"Libby, I'm so glad to see you safe and sound." He pulled me into his arms and squeezed me tight.

Warmth filled my chest, and I rested my head on his shoulder, savoring the comfort of his embrace. I was so fortunate to be in a relationship with such an amazing, caring man. Was my worry about meeting his parents simply an expression of some deep-down fear that I wasn't worthy of his love?

Quite possibly, given how things had ended with my ex-husband.

"My mom texted this morning," Sam said as he stepped back. "They're leaving at three and should be here in plenty of time to go to dinner. I've made reservations at La Villetta."

"Yum. The best place in town." I squashed down my insecurities and reminded myself how much I liked La Villetta's food.

"I took them there when they last came to visit me, not long before I met you. They loved it."

Although Sam's parents lived less than two hours away in St. Louis, his dad had gone through some health issues last summer, and Sam had other family in St. Louis, so he went there more often than his parents visited Dogwood Springs.

Bella, who for once had been patient, wriggled her body between us and barked at Sam.

He laughed and followed me into my apartment, where

he knelt on the floor and gave Bella some attention. She rested a paw on one of his shoulders and licked his cheek.

"Bella," I laughingly scolded.

Sam scratched between her ears, then stood. "No worries. She's just trying to remind me that she's my best girl." He winked at me. "Ready to go?"

I picked up Bella's leash and my purse.

Soon we were settled in Sam's car with Bella in the back on a stadium blanket.

A few minutes later Sam parked in front of a cute little shop with a bright purple awning a block off Main Street.

I started to let Bella out but hesitated. "Are you sure she can come in?"

"I'll double-check." Sam walked up the path of pavers, knocked, and stepped inside. A moment later he came back out, pointed at Bella, and gestured for both of us to come in.

"Let's go, girl." I clipped on her leash and followed her up the pathway.

Sam held the door open, and Bella and I went in.

A woman in her late forties with shoulder-length blond curls rose from behind a desk. She wore a loose, teal linen dress, tan sandals, and a colorful necklace made of ceramic beads. "Libby, I'm so glad to meet you. And glad to meet Bella as well. I'm Adrienne." She stepped around the edge of the desk and held out her hand for Bella to sniff.

Bella licked it, and Adrienne giggled.

"Come." She beckoned us through her workspace, which was piled with sample books, and toward her back door. "It's still cool out. Let's sit on my patio."

The concrete slab patio had been painted in a large black-and-white checkerboard pattern. A black metal table and chairs sat on one end of a hot-pink outdoor rug, and two black metal chairs with hot-pink floral cushions sat on the other. A water feature gurgled at the edge of the patio, and three hummingbird feeders hanging from a nearby tree were abuzz with activity.

She encouraged Sam and me to take the cushioned chairs and pulled over a chair from the dining table for herself. Bella plopped down by Sam, her eyes on the hummingbirds.

"Thanks for talking with us, Adrienne," Sam said.

She chuckled. "For one of my best customers? Any time. What can I help you with?"

I explained about the letter we'd found in the secret compartment in the bookcase, giving Sam full credit for discovering the hiding places.

Adrienne flattened a hand against her chest. "So not just the liquor cubbies, but two more hiding spots?"

Sam nodded.

"Ooh, I love it! And it's another historical mystery for you all to solve!" She leaned toward me. "Sam's told me all about you and Bella and the mystery of the girl in the painting. So incredibly cool."

Bella stood and put her head on Sam's knee.

He scratched her ears and turned to Adrienne. "Do you remember where you got the bookcase?"

"I bought it locally, from an antique dealer who runs the Yesterday's Treasures shop out near that historic orchard southwest of town." Adrienne pulled her phone from a side pocket on her skirt. "I think she's on a buying trip, but I can give you her number."

A second later, Sam's phone dinged with an incoming message.

"Do you mind if I call now?" he asked Adrienne.

She made a hurry-up motion with one hand. "Please, go ahead. I can't wait to hear what you learn."

Sam put his phone on speaker and dialed.

There was a long delay, and then he left a message.

I let out a long sigh. "I hate waiting."

"Yeah, me too," Adrienne said. "But I can tell you one bit of good news. I'm almost certain the dealer told me she bought that bookcase at an estate sale here in town."

"In town?" Sam and I said in unison.

The three of us laughed.

"That's excellent news." I grabbed Sam's arm. "We might be able to find the fireplace where the diary was hidden. Of course, it may not be there anymore ..."

"But you never know," Sam said.

We thanked Adrienne for her help, promised to keep her posted on what we learned, and climbed back into Sam's car.

I fastened my seat belt. "I shouldn't be so impatient. When we tried to learn more about the girl painted out of that family portrait, it didn't happen overnight."

"True. I guess we'll have to while away the time eating at La Villetta," Sam said.

"Oh, yeah." I gave him my best I'm-not-nervous smile. "Sounds delicious."

He drove Bella and me to the tire shop, and soon I was home, staring at my closet, trying to decide what to wear to dinner.

Chapter Seventeen

FINALLY, after changing my mind five times about what to wear to dinner, I went back to the outfit I'd originally picked: black cotton pants and a short-sleeved, emerald-green sweater.

Normally, I wasn't so wishy-washy. Was it all my nervousness about meeting Sam's parents? Or was it also the fact that a double murderer might have slashed my tires the previous day?

I'd just gotten dressed when Cleo called out hello and knocked on my front door.

"How are you doing?" she asked when I let her in.

"Most of the day, I've managed to keep my mind on other things," I said. "Being targeted by a murderer does tend to distract you from the fact that you're about to meet your boyfriend's parents."

She winced. "Yeah, I guess it would." She narrowed her eyes at me, then gave a quick nod. "Your outfit is darling."

"Thanks."

She followed me into the kitchen while I fed Bella, then to my bedroom where she watched as I contemplated two pairs of shoes and decided on a simple pair of black flats. "Do you want me to do your hair and makeup?"

"Oh, you're kind to offer, but I think I should do it." Having a best friend who ran a salon certainly came in handy for special events, but Cleo would use a lot more makeup than I would. Plus, if things went well with Sam's parents, I couldn't ask her to do my hair and makeup every time I saw them in the future. "I want them to meet the real me."

Cleo hugged me. "How can you even wonder about them liking you? You're so sweet and authentic."

"Thanks." Hopefully sweet and authentic was enough. I really, really didn't want them to think I was only dating Sam for his money. "Would you be willing to keep me company, though, while I'm getting ready?"

"I'd be happy to." She sat down on the couch facing the door to my bathroom and, in a series of loud, funny stories, told me about the clients she'd seen that day.

Finally, at five minutes till six, I was ready.

"You're going to do great and—"

Her phone dinged with a text. She pulled it from her pocket and her face lit up. "They accepted my offer!" She let out a squeal. "I'm going to own the salon!"

"Oh, Cleo, that's fabulous!" I hugged her. "Congratulations!"

"I've got to call my real estate agent to thank her for all

her help." Cleo fluffed one side of my hair with her fingers and dashed upstairs.

Cleo's excitement woke Bella, who had begun to doze. She joined me as I peeked out the living room window and nuzzled her leg against my black pants, leaving a fine coating of golden dog hair.

"Not the best time for dog hair, Bella." I dashed into the kitchen, grabbed a dog biscuit, and set it on the floor in front of the fireplace. Then I got out my lint roller.

I was still cleaning my pant legs when I heard a knock at the outer front door.

Bella lurched to her feet and beat me to the door to the entryway, eager to greet whoever had come to visit. When I let Sam in, she let out a woof and danced in excited circles around him.

"Libby." Sam took my hands. "You look gorgeous."

"Thank you." I looked him up and down, admiring his thick, dark hair, the line of his jaw, and his dark jeans, dress shirt, and loafers.

He bent down to talk to Bella. "And you, my darling, are such a good girl. We're going to have to plan a Frisbee date soon. I can't take you to La Villetta, but next time my parents are in town, they can meet you." He stood and turned to me. "Are you ready?"

I grabbed my purse from my living room. "Sure. I don't want to keep your parents waiting."

I gave Bella one more pat and walked with Sam out to where he'd parked on Elm Street.

A woman with a round face and short, fluffy brown hair waved at me through the rear window.

The front passenger seat was empty, and Sam opened the door.

"Would one of you prefer to sit in the front?" I asked his parents, who were both in the back seat.

"No, we're fine," Sam's mom said. "We're so happy to meet you, Libby. I'm Donna, and this is Rich." She gestured to the man beside her. He looked much as I'd imagined Sam would when he was older—the same handsome face, dark hair with a sprinkle of gray, and the same chocolate brown eyes.

"It's nice to meet you both," I said as I climbed in.

Five minutes later, we were parked in the lot behind La Villetta. Once everyone got out, I was able to get a better look at Sam's parents.

Rich was shorter than Sam and a bit heavier. He wore tan microfiber pants and a navy polo.

Donna was about my height, slightly plump, and had a kind smile. She wore navy polyester pants and a tunic in shades of blue and turquoise.

"What a pretty blouse," I said. "I just love it."

Her smile deepened, and her eyes sparkled. "I'm so glad. I've worried for days about what to wear tonight. I've been so nervous about meeting you."

"You've been nervous?" I stared at her. "I've been worried about this for weeks, afraid you'll think I'm only interested in Sam for his money." I gulped. Had I said that out loud? I shot a glance at Sam.

"Oh, Libby." Donna leaned closer to pat my arm, and I caught a faint hint of her floral perfume. "Sam's assured us that he has no worries on that account." She lowered her voice. "I guess after that last woman he dated—you know about her?" Donna raised an eyebrow.

I nodded.

"I guess he learned to listen to his intuition," she said.

"Mo-om," Sam said in mock annoyance. "I'm right here, and I can hear every word you're saying."

I stifled a giggle. I couldn't help it. Sam was thirty-eight, worth half a billion dollars, and he sounded like he was in high school.

Donna rolled her eyes. "I only want Libby to know she doesn't need to worry. A mother can tell when one of her children is truly happy. Dating Libby has been good for you." She patted Sam's shoulder, then beamed at me.

"It seems like I'm the one who should have been worried," Sam muttered to his dad. "Next thing you know, Mom will bring out photos of me from when I had braces."

The four of us laughed. Tension melted from my shoulders, and we walked through the alley, around to the front of La Villetta.

The minute we entered the building, the rich aroma of garlic, onions, tomatoes, and cheese surrounded us. I could even smell fresh bread baking.

Rich inhaled deeply. "I love this place."

"Me too," I agreed.

Not only did La Villetta have the best gourmet food in town, but it also managed to walk a fine line between classy and casual. It was one of those restaurants with chande-liers, candles shining on every table, and gleaming glass-ware that made you feel like you could relax and be pampered. But an occasional burst of laughter rose above the quiet conversation, and a swath of butcher paper topped with crayons was spread across every table. It was clear it welcomed any guest, even tourists who'd only packed jeans when they came to Dogwood Springs.

The service was timely, and soon we were munching on crusty bread and tasting our salads. I'd opted for one topped with blue cheese crumbles, sliced pears, walnuts, and a light, fruity dressing while Sam and his parents had all chosen the Caesar.

Sam filled his parents in on the new business he was starting and promised his mom that he wasn't going to be too busy with the business and teaching. "It's a small start-up, Mom. Once I get things organized, I'll hire someone to handle the day-to-day operations."

She seemed a bit hesitant to believe him, but her brow eased when he mentioned that he wanted to have plenty of time to spend with me.

"I knew you were good for him." She beamed at me.

For a few minutes, the conversation lagged, and my mind wandered back to the remaining suspects in the murder. If the killer wasn't Noreen or Edna, that only left Chip, Gene, or Trent. But could I rule out Noreen and Edna completely?

The server returned with our dinners, and I drew my attention back to the meal. Sam and his dad had both chosen the seafood ravioli. His mom had gone for the day's special, a chicken breast covered in an artichoke spread with a side of mushroom risotto. I'd stuck with my old favorite, spaghetti and meatballs.

Not every restaurant could make a proper Italian meatball, but La Villetta could. Moist, perfectly seasoned, and held together with a rich parmesan.

"Sam tells us that you're investigating two mysteries right now," Rich said.

"We are." Between us, Sam and I explained how we'd discovered the letter, pointing to the diary, in the hidden compartment in the antique bookcase.

"We tried to contact the antique dealer who sold the bookcase to Sam's interior designer," I said, "but she was out of town."

"I'm still waiting for her to get in touch," Sam said.

"What about the murders Sam mentioned?" Donna's eyes tensed. "Have the police arrested anyone yet?"

"No. The detective in charge got hung up initially suspecting a woman who's fairly new to Dogwood Springs. I only hope he's moved on." I described all that Valerie had gone through with the fire out west and losing her husband. "She doesn't have a reason to kill Patti Sue or Jade. She only seems suspicious because she found Patti Sue's body."

"Sam's told us about the mysteries you've solved in the past," Donna said. "You've got a gift for figuring out puzzles, Libby, but I hope you're being careful when you talk to possible murder suspects." There was a note in Donna's voice that made me think she'd probably worry as much as my own mom if she knew what I'd been doing and—

My mouth went dry. What if she was afraid that dating me was dangerous for Sam because I kept getting involved in murder investigations? That was even worse than if I was dating him for his money.

"I'm always careful." I tried to sound reassuring. No way was I mentioning the fact that my tires had been slashed.

"I imagine, Donna," Rich added gently, "that Libby can learn a lot by talking with people who weren't directly involved in the murder. Friends of suspects, people like that."

Sam and I both quickly agreed. I changed the subject to ask about his parents' life back in St. Louis, and Rich began to tell us about their plan to get a new puppy.

We had a long discussion about the puppy, about the golden retriever they had owned when Sam was a boy, and about Bella. Before I knew it, we'd finished dessert.

Sam drove me back to my apartment, stepped into the entryway with me, and drew me into his arms.

"Wait." I held a hand against his chest. "Do your parents worry about your safety if you're getting involved in murder investigations because of me?"

Sam tilted his head to one side and stared at me. "How did you get that idea?"

"Your mom seemed worried about me, and you're her son, and ..."

He shook his head. "Even if we investigated another ten

murders, Mom knows I'll be careful. Her big fear was always related to the traffic in California."

"Oh." I let out a ragged breath.

"They loved you," he whispered in my ear. "Almost as much as I do."

My heart tingled, and I hugged him tight. "All that worry." I laughed. "And it turned out just fine." I slid my fingers into the hair at the nape of his neck and raised my lips to his.

He kissed me, paused, and then kissed me again. "I've got to drive them back to my place." He caught my hands in his. "But, man, I hate to leave."

"Well, let's just say you owe me about ten more kisses." I grinned at him.

"That's an IOU that I'll look forward to paying." He squeezed my hands and slipped out the door.

I let out an enormous sigh. Dinner had gone well. Sam's parents loved me. And he loved me. I closed my eyes and stood there, sinking back into the sensation of his arms around me and his heart beating next to mine.

Then I smiled and thought about those other kisses he owed me.

I couldn't wait to collect.

Chapter Eighteen

AFTER I LET Bella out in the backyard for a few minutes, I put on my pajamas and started to get ready for bed. But I had this weird feeling I'd missed something.

Nope. Couldn't figure out what it was.

Only when I was brushing my teeth, with my mouth full of minty toothpaste, did I remember.

Sam's dad had mentioned talking not only to suspects but to people around them. Maybe we hadn't done enough of that. A friend or casual acquaintance might be more likely to divulge a key clue than an actual suspect.

Normally I counted on Alice and Cleo for insider information about people in Dogwood Springs. They'd lived here far longer than me and had more connections. But I'd been here more than a year now. Maybe I knew someone.

I ran through our list of remaining suspects—Noreen, Edna, Chip, Trent, and Gene. Who did I know who might have information about one of them?

I flossed my teeth, thinking of my local connections.

And stopped with the floss between my bottom front teeth.

Dallas McAllister.

Dallas, the wife of Sam's department chair, was a surgical nurse at the hospital. She might know more about Noreen through the hospital and more about Chip through her husband's job. And although she could talk non-stop, Dallas was also genuinely interested in other people.

It was close to ten, but I remembered Sam mentioning a donor recognition banquet tonight at the university that he'd avoided because only department chairs and upper administration were expected to attend. Dallas was bound to still be awake. I sent her a text, and she replied within less than a minute.

We made plans to meet for lunch the next day at the Pit & Pickle Barbecue Joint.

"Libby!" From the far side of the Pit & Pickle dining room the next day, Dallas stood and waved. A tall, attractive Black woman, she was hard to miss in her bright-orange shirt and vivid green pants.

I made my way through the crowd near the door and sat in the booth across from her.

"I got here a few minutes early and put my name in. I hope you don't mind that I went ahead and sat down," she said.

"Not at all. I'm thrilled you got a spot, and I'm so glad you could meet me." I smiled at her.

A few seconds later, a server approached our table and took our drink orders.

I glanced at the menu and set it aside. I'd be hard-pressed not to order onion rings since I could smell some from the next table over.

The Pit & Pickle, which had opened three months ago, was near the university and had become one of my favorite places to meet Sam for lunch. It had a comfortable retro feel with black vinyl booths, shiny wooden tables, and paneled walls lined with antique metal advertising signs. Above our table was a large sign for Sun Drop soda.

"Let's see." Dallas studied the menu, then her eyes lit, and she placed the menu on the table. "For a minute there I couldn't find my favorite." She shifted in her seat and continued in a lower voice. "You said there were five people who could have killed Patti Sue?"

I leaned in so I could better hear her over the crowd and filled her in on what we'd learned so far about Trent, Noreen, Edna, Chip, and Gene.

She leaned in, listening intently.

But when I started to tell her about the conversation Sam and I had with Chip on campus, her expression changed. "Wait. First of all, Chip is seriously underplaying how hard it is to hire a lab manager who wants to move to Dogwood Springs. And if a technical position like that stays vacant, a faculty member can fail to meet all the deliverables for their research grants. But the bigger question is, what about the affair?"

I sat up taller. "What affair?"

"Let me text a friend to check something." Dallas pulled out her phone and began rapidly texting, her hot-pink fingernails glinting in the overhead light.

Curiosity welled up inside me. "Chip was—?"

The server chose that exact moment to come back with our drinks and take our lunch orders. I ordered as fast as I could, dying to know more.

Finally, he closed his notepad and walked away.

I frantically motioned for Dallas to spill what she knew.

She chuckled. "It's only a rumor." She took a quick drink of her soda. "But I've heard that Chip is having an affair with Louella Bradley."

Her phone dinged with a text and almost immediately dinged again.

"Oh, this might be the answer to my question." She bent down to read her phone. "Aha! Just as I thought. Louella lives at Hartley Road Apartments."

I leaned forward and laid both hands flat on the table. "Which Patti Sue owned and where Jade was the assistant manager. Either one of them, or both of them, could have seen Chip at the apartment complex and figured out what was going on."

"If Patti Sue knew about that affair, she'd make Chip and Louella's lives miserable."

"Blackmail?" I asked.

"No, I can't see her trying to blackmail someone." Dallas

tapped a fingernail on the table. "How to explain it? She enjoyed the power, the feeling of being able to grind someone into the dirt. Not something I see Chip enjoying one bit."

I thought back to the undercurrent of ego I'd felt when I met him. "No," I said, "I can't imagine him enjoying that either. He seems like a very strong suspect." More so than Edna or Trent or Gene or Noreen.

Dallas's eyes clouded. "You'll be careful, won't you, Libby?"

"I will," I promised. "And I'll take Sam with me."

She let out a slow, satisfied breath. "That sounds smart." She picked up her soda cup and her eyes twinkled. "Now, I heard you had dinner last night with Sam and his parents at La Villetta. A friend of mine was sitting two tables over. Sounds like things are getting more serious."

"I, um, I enjoyed meeting his parents," I said. "They're nice people."

And that was all I wanted to reveal, no matter how much Dallas pried.

Call me hypocritical, but although I found it very convenient when I was investigating a mystery that everyone in a small town knew everyone else's business, I was enough of a city girl that I wasn't quite used to everyone knowing *my* business.

Luckily, the server returned with my heaping plate of barbecued brisket and onion rings and Dallas's barbecued chicken sandwich and fries, and I was able to divert the conversation to other topics.

As soon as I got home from lunch, I called Sam and told him what I'd learned from Dallas.

The next day was the start of the fall semester, which Sam said was bound to be hectic, but he promised to try to figure out a way we could talk with Chip. Our conversation was short as he was struggling to upload a syllabus to the campus system, which kept crashing.

The next morning, Rodney was delayed in returning from the wedding because his flight was canceled. So Imani and I had our regular Monday morning meeting with muffins, saving one for him, and then we prepared to hold down the fort with the help of three volunteers.

I was just heading up to my office when I got a text from Sam.

The administrator for the computer science department where Sam worked was friends with the administrator for the biology department where Chip worked. According to the biology staffer, unless there was a departmental function that involved free food, Chip ate at his desk. She even checked Chip's schedule and told us when he had a lunch break.

Sam had a small window that overlapped, so I got directions from him as to the best place to park as a visitor on campus. I agreed to meet him outside the biology building at a quarter after twelve.

The rest of the morning zipped by. I ate lunch early at my desk, ran home to feed Bella and let her out, and then drove south to Grove University. Soon I was wandering on campus, trying to figure out which of the red brick buildings housed the biology department. After a few minutes, I broke down, used the map app on my phone, and followed a sidewalk west.

"Libby." Sam waved.

I slid my phone into my purse. "Hi, Sam. Thanks for meeting me. Ready to talk to Chip?"

"You bet," Sam said. "After what Dallas told you yesterday, he seems like a very strong suspect. And I don't want you talking to him alone." He stopped at one of the red brick buildings, we went in, and he led me down the hall to the right.

A few seconds later, he stopped beside a door. A small sign beside it identified it as Chip's office.

I glanced at Sam and knocked.

There was a garbled response that sounded something like "Come in."

I tentatively pushed the door open.

Chip sat at his desk. His jacket was tossed on a nearby table, and he looked more harried than he had when we talked with him at the amphitheater. That may have been because it was the first day of class, or it may have been because his office was about ninety degrees.

A flicker of surprise shot through Chip's eyes, but he rapidly regained his composure. "I apologize for the heat in here. The AC is on the fritz. Did you talk to Gene about inheriting the apartment complex when Patti Sue died? Does it seem like he's the killer?"

"Not particularly." Sam closed the office door. "But it does seem like you left a lot out when you spoke with us the other day, like how hard it can be to hire a lab manager. Having Patti Sue drive away that candidate must have you scrambling to deliver on your research contracts."

Chip's face reddened. "So, I downplayed it a little. It's only because you two were totally on the wrong track. There's no way I would kill someone over a hiring situation."

Through the wall, I heard a phone ring in the office next door.

I took a step closer. "What about someone who threatened to divulge that you're having an affair?"

He leapt to his feet, his hands tightening into fists. "Keep your voice down. These walls are paper thin." He glared at me. "My personal life is none of your business. And I did not kill Patti Sue Harrison."

Sam stood taller and shot Chip a look that had him uncurling his fists.

"But you are having an affair with someone who lives at Hartley Road Apartments," I said more quietly.

"I am," he admitted, "but I don't think Patti Sue knew about it." He winced. "If she had, she'd have told the whole town."

"It does make you seem suspicious, Chip," Sam said.

"Yeah, it does." He ran his hands down his pant legs. "But I didn't kill her. What, you think I just walked down the hallway at the high school and strangled her?"

"Somebody did," I said.

"I've got two things to tell you. First of all, keep quiet about my personal life, and whoever told you, tell them to shut up." His nostrils flared. "Second, if I had wanted to kill Patti Sue, I wouldn't have done something as clumsy as strangling her. You can't work in biology at the level I do without a deep understanding of chemistry. If I wanted someone dead, I'd poison them, and no one would ever have a clue."

A shiver ran down my spine, and I glanced at Sam.

He narrowed his eyes at Chip. "Good to know." Sam took my elbow and guided me out of Chip's office, shutting the door behind him.

Once we were in the hall, we hurried to the main door and burst outside.

"Holy cow." I let out a long breath.

"Man, I'm glad he's not in my department."

"I believe him, though. I don't think he was the person who strangled Patti Sue."

"No, I don't think he was either," Sam said. "I think we can take him off the suspect list. And the guest list for any future dinner parties."

I shuddered and nodded.

Sam walked me to my car. "You doing all right?" he asked when we reached the parking lot.

"Yeah, I guess, but I sure wish we could figure this out," I replied. "If Chip isn't the murderer, then who is? Somebody has to be lying, but I can't figure out who it is."

"You'll get there," Sam said.

"I hope so." I kissed him goodbye and got in my car,

grateful for the heat that had built up inside it in the August sun. I needed something to warm me up after the chill of talking to Chip.

I drove back to the museum, thinking that, ordinarily, when I counted my blessings, I didn't include the fact that I was sure neither of my colleagues had a plan at the tip of their tongue for how they might murder someone.

Next time I would.

I had just parked at the museum when my phone dinged with an incoming text. I dug it out of my purse.

Zeke Anderson
Talked to a friend and his mom. She works with Noreen. Noreen wasn't at the hospital all day on the day Jade died like she said. She took off for 2 hours for a doctor's appointment.

Oh, wow.

Noreen might have said she had a doctor's appointment and instead gone to the apartment complex and killed Jade.

So Noreen's alibi could be a big, fat lie.

A lie she could have told to cover up the fact that she was a double murderer.

Chapter Nineteen

MY MIND RACED as I went back into the museum. No matter how much I wanted to follow up on the lead about Noreen, I had work to do.

In the conference room, Imani set a large box on the table. "I decided that since so few people are visiting the museum, it would be a perfect time to assemble new member packs."

"Great idea." The supplies were all stored in the attic, so I helped her move them down.

"Here's the last one," I said fifteen minutes later, as I shifted a box from the dolly to the table in the conference room, then rubbed my lower back.

"I can't thank you enough for helping, Libby. I know there's a table up in the attic where I could have worked, but we'll need the packets down here once they're done. And it's a lot cooler on the first floor."

"Makes sense to me." The attic wasn't air-conditioned

and had to be at least twenty degrees warmer. "Mostly, I'm grateful we have the elevator now."

"You and me both," Imani said. "I—"

The back door opened, and a rather harried Rodney stepped inside.

"Well, look who finally made it in," Imani teased as she began taking brochures out of the boxes. "Right after we got done with the heavy lifting."

"Don't even start." Rodney rolled his eyes. "The wedding was fun, but the trip back was unreal. Two hours sitting in a hot plane on the tarmac and then they canceled the flight. My wife and I got the last two seats on another carrier, and she just dropped me off as we drove into town."

"That sounds awful," I said. "Are you sure you don't want to take the rest of the day off?"

"Nope." Rodney dug around in our mini fridge, pulled out a soda, and cracked it open. Carbonation fizzed. "What's new around here?"

"Nothing good." Imani gave an exaggerated shudder. "Libby left her car in the parking lot on Friday evening after the museum closed, and someone slashed her tires."

Rodney's mouth dropped open. "In our parking lot?"

"Most likely someone's unhappy that I've been asking questions about Patti Sue and Jade's murders." I didn't think the staff or volunteers of the museum were in danger. At least I hoped not.

"When exactly did this happen?" Rodney asked.

"Sometime between when Alice picked me up at five

and an hour later." I opened the box closest to me and pulled out some brochures.

"I was the last one to leave Friday," Rodney said slowly. "As I drove out of the lot, I could have sworn I saw someone hanging out in the back corner near those two trees. You know where I mean?"

Imani and I said we did.

"I thought it was weird at the time. Why would someone be standing out there in the rain? But with all that went on this weekend, I had forgotten about it."

"Did you see their face?" I asked.

"No. But whoever it was had on an orange ball cap and an orange T-shirt."

The image clicked into place in my brain. "Like the people who work at Green Thumb Greenhouse. Like Trent Miles, who's one of our suspects."

"Rodney, you need to tell the police," Imani said. "Trent may have waited around until you left and then committed the crime."

"I don't know," I said. "Would you really wear bright orange to commit a crime?"

"You might if you wore it all the time," Imani said. "Once I had a part-time job at Gerry's Hot Dogs. I had to wear this stupid hat, and at first, I thought about it all the time, but eventually, I didn't even notice," she explained. "So maybe Trent's the same with the orange shirt and hat."

"Maybe," I said.

"I'll go call the police right now." Rodney stepped into the hallway.

A couple of minutes later, he returned, looking just as annoyed as he had when he described his plane trip.

"Was Detective Harper out of the office?" I asked.

"He was there," Rodney said. "And he thanked me for the information. But he didn't act like the clue was any big deal. I got the impression he didn't suspect Trent at all."

I shook my head. "Never mind, Rodney. I'll check it out. I think it's a valuable lead."

I followed Rodney up the stairs and was stepping into my office when my phone rang with a call from Alice.

"Hey, Alice, how was your first day of the fall semester?"

"Well, I feel old enough to be a mother to most of the students, but other than that, it was fine. I only got lost once, and the regular freshmen were quite accepting of a fellow student who's in her fifties."

"Of course they were. They may be young, but they're not stupid. They can recognize what a wonderful person you are."

"Oh, hush." Alice chuckled. "I talked to my real estate agent friend about that question you had. She hadn't heard anything about Gene wanting to sell Hartley Road Apartments, but she did know something about Trent."

"Trent?" I sat down and filled her in on the conversation I'd had with Rodney and Imani.

"Well, then, get this," Alice said. "Back when Patti Sue's husband was still alive, he made a verbal agreement to sell a strip of property between the apartment complex and Green Thumb Gardens to Trent. Apparently, Trent thought he needed more plant inventory to make a go of it, but without the extra land, he didn't have space for another greenhouse."

"I could see that." The business had seemed small, at least compared to other greenhouses I'd seen.

"But when Patti Sue's husband died," Alice continued, "she refused to honor the agreement. Trent was furious."

"Wow." I sat back in my chair. "Not only does he look like the person who slashed my tires, he's also got a really solid motive for wanting Patti Sue dead."

"Exactly," Alice agreed.

"I think I need to have another chat with Trent," I said.

"When are you planning to go? I need to read three chapters but—"

"I'll call Sam." I knew Alice well enough to know that she'd be stressed to start the semester feeling behind. If any of her professors had posted a syllabus online, she'd probably already started on the first homework assignment, even if it wasn't due until next week.

"Good idea," Alice said.

I hung up the phone with Alice and called Sam, who agreed to pick me up shortly after five.

Detective Harper might not suspect Trent, but I sure did.

By the end of the day, a thunderstorm had popped up. As I dashed out to my car in the museum parking lot, the wind whipped my hair in front of my face, and my umbrella was useless. The rain was coming down sideways.

I drove home, let Bella out, then dried her off and filled her food bowl. I thought about drying my hair before Sam picked me up but knew it would be a waste of time. Instead, I pulled it in a ponytail, put on jeans and tennis shoes, and found my rain slicker with a hood.

I watched for Sam's car to pull up in front of the house and, when he started to get out, held up a hand to stop him. I hurried out, avoided a giant puddle on the sidewalk, and climbed in. "No need for you to get out and get wet," I said.

He gestured to his shirt and khaki pants. "I'm not sure I can be any wetter. Not after walking across campus to my car."

When Sam turned into Green Thumb Gardens, the parking lot was empty. We dashed to the door and stood inside for a moment, dripping on a mat by the door.

Wind whipped rain against the windows so hard that I checked to be sure it wasn't hail.

"Good for you braving this weather." Trent, who seemed to be working alone, stepped out from behind the counter. "What can I help you with today?"

While it made sense that a gardener wouldn't want to take home a tender plant on a day with forty-mile-an-hour winds, the fact that the store was empty, except for Sam, Trent, and me, was a little eerie. And the room felt different without any sunshine coming through the windows. I shot a glance at Sam, grateful he'd come with me.

"Actually, we came to talk with you again." I walked toward the counter. "You didn't tell us the whole story when we were here last time, did you?"

Trent edged back and leaned his hips against the counter. "What do you mean?"

I'd expected some defensiveness, but as last time, he seemed almost overly eager to please.

"I mean you had a very strong reason to want Patti Sue dead in addition to how she bad-mouthed your lawn care business." I kept my gaze steady, willing him to break down and tell the truth. "From what I hear, if your business is going to be successful, you need to add another greenhouse. The land that Patti Sue's husband had agreed to sell you was vital for that expansion."

Sam took a step closer to Trent. "But after her husband died, Patti Sue didn't uphold his verbal agreement. She refused to sell."

"Having her destroy your first business and then stand in the way of your second business certainly could have made you hate her," I said. "Especially after the money you and your wife had invested. Maybe it made you mad enough to kill her."

Trent shrugged. "It could have, but it didn't. Am I glad she's dead? Yeah. Will my life be a lot easier? Yes again. I'm sure Gene will be happy to sell me that strip of land. It has no real value to the apartment complex. But did I kill her? No."

No matter how nice he acted—and I really thought it was an act—Trent's motive sounded stronger and stronger.

I planted my hands on my hips. "But—"

"If I wanted her dead," Trent interrupted, "would I have rescued her a week before she died?"

"Rescued her?" My hands dropped to my sides. "How did you rescue her?"

"I think it was the Tuesday before she died, I went over to try to get her to realize that it didn't make sense to keep that little strip of property just to thwart me. The cash would help her business. She could have used it to do some maintenance around the apartments, you know?"

He gazed at me as if expecting a reply, so I dipped my chin in acknowledgment.

"She was trying to get stuff done, and I followed her around as we talked. The office building is different from the others in the complex. It's like an apartment on one side and the other side is the laundry room. And it has a full basement instead of a crawl space. I think it was designed as a tornado shelter."

"That makes sense with how many tornados Missouri has," Sam said.

Trent nodded and continued. "While we were talking, Patti Sue walked back toward the utility room, and then she lost her balance and slipped on a puddle of water on the floor. If it hadn't been for me grabbing her, she would have fallen down the steps to the basement. She would have landed on the concrete floor and probably whacked her head on the concrete wall at the base of those stairs."

I looked over at Sam. This was all news to me.

Trent spread his hands wide. "If I'd wanted the woman dead, I could have simply let her fall. I mean, I guess there's a chance she could have survived, but she was kind of a frail little thing. I imagine she'd have broken several bones at the minimum."

Which would have landed her in the hospital, I thought, where she'd have been very vulnerable if someone wanted to smother her with a pillow.

"But boy, oh boy, you should have heard her." Trent planted one hand on a hip. "She was so peeved with her brother-in-law, saying he should have done a better job dealing with the leak that created the water on the floor. To hear her tell it, the leak was worse after he'd worked on the water heater than before."

"Now, that's interesting," I said.

"It sure is," Sam agreed. "Did you tell the police about the leak and the wet spot on the floor, Trent?"

"Nah, I didn't think of it when the cops were here. Do you think it's important?" His eyes narrowed as if he might be putting together the puzzle and seeing the same picture we had.

"It might be," I said.

"I'll call them now." He pulled his phone out of his pocket.

"Good idea. I think that's all the questions I have." I edged toward the door. "Sorry to have bothered you."

"It's okay," he said. "I understand you need this thing solved to help your museum. I might do the same thing if it was my business that was having trouble. But you've got to believe me. I didn't kill her."

I looked him in the eye. "I do believe you, Trent." I hadn't at first, but I did now. I pulled up my hood and zipped my rain jacket, and Sam and I dashed back to his car.

Sam drove through the pouring rain back to my apartment, and I sat silent the whole way, thinking.

Chapter Twenty

THE NEXT DAY, I took my car to work. Just after eleven, I drove home, let Bella out, gobbled down a peanut butter and jelly sandwich, and then headed to the police station.

Inside the station, the air conditioning was wheezing but valiantly pouring out cool air. The desk sergeant appeared to be watching a video on his phone about how to change the brake pads on his car.

I hitched my purse up higher on my shoulder, approached him, introduced myself, and asked to speak to Detective Harper.

The sergeant silenced the volume on his video but didn't turn it off. "He's out of town, ma'am." He glanced at the door as if hoping I'd leave, then looked back at his phone.

Drat. Detective Harper was probably at another one of those training seminars in St. Louis.

I searched my brain and came up with the name of the detective who had talked with me when I'd found Jade's body. "Could I speak with Detective Sanders, then? I have information about the recent murders here in town. I've, uh, I've got a theory I want to share."

The sergeant made a face like he'd just learned that brake pads were out of stock across the country, and he shut off his phone. "Sanders isn't available right now."

Hmmm. "What about Officer Tate?" He seemed like the most senior of the uniformed officers I'd met.

"He's out on patrol." The sergeant pulled out a pencil and paper. "I can take your name and number. Detective Sanders will call you when he's free."

"But—"

"Lib-by," he said slowly as he wrote. "Spell your last name, please."

I blew out a long breath. "Fine." I spelled out *Ballard*, gave him my cell number, and headed to the museum.

Surely Detective Sanders would call soon.

Nope.

One o'clock passed.

Two o'clock.

Three.

And with every hour my jaw grew tighter.

Finally, I spun my desk chair to face the window, crossed my arms over my chest, and sat there, thinking. If Detective Harper was in St. Louis, he wasn't going to solve this case. And Detective Sanders—if he ever called me back —hadn't inspired confidence from either Cleo or me.

Somebody needed to stop the killer.

Luckily, I had a plan.

Right after five o'clock, I told Imani and Rodney goodbye and locked the museum doors. Then I texted Sam, Alice, Cleo, and Zeke to let them know that Step One of my plan was in motion.

I walked home, took care of Bella, and microwaved a frozen dinner. Once I'd eaten and changed into shorts and a T-shirt, I took Bella's leash off the hook on the kitchen wall.

"Ready to help me catch a killer, girl?"

She gave an excited woof, and the two of us walked to the museum.

After we arrived, I turned on all the lights to make myself less nervous. Then I had a chat with Bella about the fact that she was to sit quietly on the doormat near the museum entrance and not disturb the displays. There had been a time in the past when she'd chewed on a boot in a display. After that incident, I normally only allowed Bella in my office, and only when the museum was closed.

Next, I prepared my trap. In one of the main first-floor display spaces, an area under the upstairs women's bathroom, I cleared a spot on the floor, shifting items to the far end of the room. I moved a whole pile of period furniture and other artifacts from the family home of a man who ran a local lumber business around 1900. That included a caned-back chair, a charming little walnut table, a gas lamp, the antique parasol Rodney had repaired, records from the lumber business, some period sheet music, and a settee, which was way heavier than I expected.

Bella came with me as I got a sponge mop and bucket out of the closet in the conference room. I put enough water in the bucket to wet my mop and carried it into the display space.

Bella watched, head cocked to one side, as I carefully dampened the mop and used it to make an irregularly shaped watermark on the ceiling directly below that second-floor bathroom.

Then I placed the bucket, which still held about a cup of water, under the watermark, returned the mop to the closet, and assessed my work.

Not bad. To me, at least, it looked as if the upstairs plumbing was leaking.

"Show time, Bella." I pulled my phone out of my shorts pocket and dialed.

After two rings, a man answered. "Harrison Plumbing. This is Gene."

"Hi, Gene. This is Libby Ballard, from the Dogwood Springs History Museum. I've got an emergency."

If he was surprised that I called him a week after thinking he was a murderer, he didn't let on. "What's going on?"

I explained that after the museum closed for the day, I had gone by while walking my dog downtown. I stopped in to get a file I needed and heard an odd drip, which I'd eventually traced to one of the main display rooms.

"I moved the artifacts out from under the drip," I said. "But I think something must be broken in the bathroom that's right above it. I managed to turn off the water main to the building, but the spot in the ceiling is still dripping."

"I see." He was quiet a moment. "It sounds like you may have water between the floors. I can't get there for another hour and a half. I'm dealing with an emergency at the Catholic church. Move as much as you can out from under the entire area of the bathroom, just in case. I expect you want to protect your displays."

"I sure do."

"Okay, I'll be there about eight."

"Thank you." I had one more tidbit of information I needed to feed him. "I'm here alone, so please knock loudly on the back door when you arrive in case I'm still moving things and have trouble hearing you."

"Will do."

I hung up and texted my friends to tell them the second step of the plan was complete. Gene was on his way, and he knew I was alone.

Which I was, at the moment. But by the time he arrived, I'd have plenty of reinforcements to help me.

I reminded my friends to park on Main Street or one of the side streets, not in the lot behind the museum. We didn't want Gene to realize I had help. And to make sure they'd be in place when Gene arrived, I asked them to come in through the back door of the museum before seven thirty.

Everyone replied that they would be there, and Sam even said he'd get there by seven.

Gene thought he'd been so clever, disguising himself as Trent to cut my tires, but he hadn't been smart enough.

Just to be extra careful, I called Detective Harper to tell him what I was doing. He didn't answer, but I left a message.

Then I unlocked the back door, moved a couple more items from under the area of the supposed leak, and sat on a bench in the main hall, running through what I planned to say to Gene.

Bella settled down beside me, her tags jingling against the tile floor.

"Now all we do is wait, Bella. Once everyone is in place, when Gene arrives, if I can get him to confess the truth, Zeke will get an audio recording. Sam and Cleo will jump out to protect me if things get ugly. And, if Detective Harper isn't already here, Alice will be ready to call the police."

Ten minutes later, I was bored, and I still had a while to wait before Sam would arrive. I went to the restroom, rechecked the room where I'd staged the leak, and sat back down by Bella. The air conditioner kicked on, and I scooted down the bench to be directly under a vent. Then I rubbed Bella's ears and scrolled through social media while she took a nap.

A few minutes later, I heard the back door open. Sam had gotten here even earlier than he'd said.

Bella quickly rose to her feet and barked.

"Libby?" a voice called.

My heart froze.

That wasn't Sam.

Heavy footsteps came down the hallway. "I was missing a part I needed for the last job and had to make do with a temporary fix," Gene said. He walked up beside me, the red faucet logo embroidered on his overalls glinting in the overhead light. "Let's get your leak taken care of."

I took a discreet peek at my phone. Fifteen minutes before any of my friends would arrive. "Great." I faked as much enthusiasm as I could. "It's, uh, it's in here. Come on, Bella."

Normally, I'd never invite her to follow me into the display space, but I was far more afraid of Gene than I was of Bella damaging an artifact.

"You can see the leak up there." I gestured above the bucket, and my hand stopped in mid-air.

There was no wet spot on the ceiling. But how—

My pointing finger started to shake as I realized what had happened.

My fake plumbing emergency had evaporated when the air conditioning came on.

"It looks like your plumbing problem has magically gone away," Gene said with an odd note in his voice.

"I, uh, I guess turning off the water main solved the problem, at least temporarily. Let me show you the upstairs bathrooms so you can find the leak."

Gene rocked back on his heels. "Really? You want to continue this charade? Because I know there's no leak."

"Uh-uh-of course there is."

"I've worked on this building before." He gave me a look that was somewhere between pity and a question of my intelligence. "I knew you were lying the minute you said you'd shut off the water main."

Huh?

"The last time I worked here, back when Vivian was still the director, I told her I needed to replace that ancient shut-off valve. Even with a vise grip it was nearly impossible for me to turn. But she didn't want to spend the money."

My mouth went dry. Why had I placed my faith in this foolish trap I'd devised? I edged back slowly, hoping he wouldn't notice.

No such luck.

Gene lunged forward, grabbed my arm, and squeezed so hard it hurt. "So, I had to ask myself why you would fake a plumbing emergency. The only reason I could think of is your annoying sleuthing and that you had some plan to trap me into a confession. It's not happening, Libby. I hate to do this, but I'm not going to jail."

I tried to twist free, but he grabbed my other arm.

Cold sweat broke out all over my body. He was bigger than me and stronger than me. In any contest that relied solely on physical strength, I was going to lose.

I sucked in a breath and tried to sound brave. "You'll never get away with it. My friends will be here any minute."

Gene's lips twisted. "If your friends were on their way, you wouldn't look so terrified."

So much for my false bravado. "They know you're coming. You'll be the first suspect if you kill me."

"Wrong again." He let out a derisive sniff. "Father Brennan thinks I'm hard at work in the basement of the Catholic church. He has no idea I slipped out the cellar door. I'll be back there in ten minutes. What better alibi is there than the word of a priest?"

He was right. My friends would arrive too late, only to find my dead body. And he'd have the perfect alibi, which—no matter what my friends said—would confuse Detective Harper even more. Gene would never be convicted for killing Patti Sue.

Or Jade.

Or me.

Chapter Twenty-One

MY HEART FELT like it was going to pound right out of my chest.

Why hadn't I waited for Detective Harper to call me back? Why hadn't I asked my friends to come sooner? Why had I ever thought I could stop a murderer?

"Please," I begged Gene. "Go back to the church, and I'll forget you were ever here."

"You know that's not true," he said. "And don't try to drag this out by getting me to tell you why I killed Patti Sue."

I gulped back a sob. That had been exactly what I was going to do. I glanced around, hoping against hope that I'd see some miracle, some way I could survive. But all I saw was Bella, glaring at Gene, with every muscle in her body tight.

"Just know that I never meant to do any of this." Gene let out a weird cry that was half laugh, half moan. And then, although I tried everything possible to escape, he twisted so he was behind me, pulled my hands together behind my back, and slipped a rope around my throat.

How had I been so stupid? Why had I ever gotten involved? Why hadn't I—

Suddenly, Bella lunged at Gene, letting out a growl like I'd never heard her make.

"Get away, you stupid dog," Gene bellowed, and he kicked at her.

My heart tightened, but she dodged the blow. Then she dashed to his side and clamped her teeth onto his leg.

"Aaaaiiii," he screamed, and his hold on me and the rope around my neck loosened.

I twisted free, scrambled across the room, and grabbed the antique parasol. I wasn't spending another second without a weapon and—

Gene kicked at Bella again, grazed her fur, and managed to break free of her grip.

He charged at me, his face flushed, his eyes hard.

And I tightened my hands on the parasol.

I'd read about this. Could I actually do it?

I had to try.

I planted my feet, used all my strength to thrust the metal tip of the parasol at Gene's throat, and jabbed it right below his Adam's apple.

He gave a strangled cry and fell backward on the floor, writhing in pain.

"Run, Bella," I shouted.

We raced into the hall and toward the conference room with Bella barking loudly.

And I pulled open the back door and ran right into Sam's chest.

"Libby, are you okay?"

I collapsed against him and pointed back inside. "Gene was early. He attacked me."

Cleo appeared beside Sam. "Is he armed?"

"No," I said.

"Come on, Sam!" Cleo cried. The two of them ran into the museum, and I stumbled outside, leaning against the side of the museum to catch my breath. I checked on Bella, but she appeared unharmed.

A second later, a white SUV pulled into the museum parking lot, and Alice climbed out.

"Libby," she called, "what's going on?"

"Gene came early," I said. "If it wasn't for Bella, he'd have killed me. But I disabled him enough to escape, and Sam and Cleo just went inside."

"I'm calling the police." Alice pulled out her phone.

"You all can come in now," Cleo called from inside. "Gene's not going to hurt anybody."

Alice stayed on the phone with the 911 operator, and the two of us walked into the museum.

In the room where I'd set my trap, Gene lay on the floor. His hands were bound behind his back with the cord he'd used to try to strangle me, and his ankles were firmly secured with Sam's belt.

He glared at me and squirmed from side to side, but he couldn't escape.

⁓

In the distance, a siren wailed.

The police were on their way. The culprit was caught. And the adrenaline that had given me energy began to wear off.

I started shaking all over.

I pulled a chair in from the hall, positioned it where I could keep an eye on Gene, and sank into it.

Bella—my dear, brave Bella—sat down beside me and rested her head on my knee.

I kissed the top of her head and scratched around the base of her ears. "You saved me, girl. You saved me." I blinked back tears and let out a heavy sigh. She wasn't simply the best, smartest dog in town. She was also the bravest.

Oh, I'd unraveled the vital clue that Trent divulged. I'd figured out the killer. But I'd have been a goner if it hadn't been for Bella.

"Alice," I said. "Will you go outside and watch for the police and show them where we are?"

"Sure thing." She squeezed my shoulder and slipped outside.

A few minutes later the siren drew closer, and soon I heard the back door open.

"They're in here," Alice said.

Officer Davis and Officer Tate rushed into the room. After we gave a quick explanation of what happened, Officer Davis freed Gene's hands and feet and handcuffed him.

"Can you tell us the full story, Libby?" Officer Tate asked.

I explained that I had called Gene to come to the museum for a plumbing problem and that he had attacked me. "He made it clear that he was the murderer. He thought I was onto him and that he had to kill me too."

"Then how ...?" Officer Davis gestured to Gene on the floor.

"He was going to strangle me with the cord that was around his wrists," I said, "but Bella attacked him."

"Bella?" Officer Davis sounded confused.

I pointed to my wonderful dog, who sat beside me with her tongue hanging out the side of her mouth, eyes smiling as innocent as you please. "She even barked to warn me when he came into the building, but I misunderstood."

Detective Harper walked in, shaking his head. "I drive up to Jefferson City to testify in a court case being tried in another jurisdiction, and everything explodes around here. Libby, you're lucky you didn't get yourself killed."

I met his eyes. "I know."

"Calling the police before you interact with a killer doesn't make it that much safer." He gave me a stern look.

He was right. More than any other case, I knew I'd nearly died with this one. Gene had been the smartest criminal I'd gone up against.

I wasn't eager to tell him the whole story, but at the moment, I was simply glad to be alive.

"Here's to Bella, a real heroine!" Sam said the next evening as we settled into our regular outside table at the Dogwood Café.

"To Bella!" Cleo, Alice, Zeke, and Valerie all cheered.

"Who saved the day." Sam leaned down and patted her head.

I dug in my purse and brought out a treat for her.

A server came by and took our drink orders, and as soon as he left, Zeke stood and adjusted the umbrella over the table to give us all more shade. By the time he sat back down, the server had returned to distribute our drinks and take our dinner orders.

"Tell us the whole story, Libby," Valerie said as he walked away. "Did Gene kill Patti Sue to get the apartment complex?"

I looked across the table at her. Already, some of the stress from being a murder suspect had fallen away. Her eyes were less tense, her posture more relaxed. And she once again wore hyacinth blue, this time in a polo shirt.

"No," I said. "I took off work today and spent a lot of it talking with Detective Harper."

As I expected, the detective had been livid when he'd learned that I'd taken matters into my own hands and set a trap for Gene. Deep down, though, I think he grudgingly respected me, at least a little. He might not approve of the risk I'd taken, but he and I shared a key value. We both wanted justice done.

"What did he say?" Alice said.

"Gene's motive was deeper than the inheritance. He blamed Patti Sue for his brother's death, believing her constant cruelty caused his heart attack."

Cleo took a sip of her Diet Dr. Pepper. "Think of all the nasty comments she must have made to poor Arthur over the years. I'm surprised he lasted as long as he did."

"Sadly, I have to agree," Alice said.

"Once Arthur passed away, and Patti Sue took over the apartments," I explained, "Gene struggled with the fact that she did such a poor job managing the complex. It was as if she was destroying his brother's legacy."

"Almost like adding insult to injury," Sam said.

"According to Detective Harper, that was how Gene felt," I replied. "And on the day of the fashion show, when he just happened to be at the high school working on the water heater, he overheard Patti Sue going on and on, criticizing his brother."

Alice pressed her lips together and shook her head.

"That pushed him over the edge," I said. "According to Detective Harper, all the pain and grief welled up in Gene, and he lost it. He saw the scarf, scooped it up, and before he even realized what he was doing, he'd killed his sister-in-law."

"Wow." Zeke studied his straw wrapper, scrunched it

into a tiny ball and, after a moment, looked back up. "He worked on our kitchen faucet. He seemed nice."

"He *was* nice," Alice agreed. "I've had him in my own home. I guess his grief, combined with Patti Sue's cruelty, changed him."

"Once he realized what he'd done," I said, "he felt guilty, but he managed to justify killing Patti Sue by telling himself that no one liked her. Then he spoke with Jade one day, and she figured out he was the murderer. He panicked, terrified that he'd end up in jail, and he killed her too."

Sam ran a hand over his chin. "Well, I don't see how he can avoid jail at this point."

The rest of us nodded. The retirement Gene had envisioned, spending all his time fishing, was never going to happen.

Zeke took a long drink and set down his soda. "How did you figure it out, Libby?"

"It was a few things. First of all, Gene was there in the hallway at the high school. He had opportunity. He also had a long history with Patti Sue, and he admitted that he'd never liked her. Then there was a comment Alice made after we'd talked to Edna about her son. She said people will do anything for their family. That stuck in my brain. And when Trent told us that Gene made the leak at the apartment office worse instead of better, especially when he was so well-respected as a plumber, and that Patti Sue almost fell down a flight of stairs to land on a concrete floor, it all made sense."

"Very logical," Alice said. "And very sad. Gene started

out as a decent man. But he was hit so hard by losing his wife and his brother that he made some bad choices."

We all sat for a moment. I, for one, had a hard time processing how fast things had spiraled out of control for Gene.

"Speaking of bad choices, I learned something at the university," Sam said. "Apparently, Chip's wife overheard him on the phone with the woman he was having an affair with. She's asking for a divorce."

I thought back to how egotistical Chip had seemed and to his comments about how he could commit a murder and get away with it. Personally, I thought his wife was making a very wise decision. The man gave me the creeps.

Zeke sat up taller. "I learned more about Noreen. She didn't want to go into detail about what she was doing on the day of Jade's murder. She was afraid her boss might learn that she wasn't at a doctor's appointment. She was interviewing for another job."

"I heard Trent is probably going to get to buy the land between his greenhouse and Hartley Road Apartments," Alice said. "I don't know if Gene can still inherit if he's found guilty, but if not, the apartments will go to Bobbi Sue. Trent thinks he can convince her to sell."

Bobbi Sue was such a nice woman that I couldn't imagine her refusing.

"And I saw Edna the other day," Alice added. "In spite of her worry, things seem to be going well for both her and her son. He's getting the treatment he needs, and she's found that the people of Dogwood Springs are more supportive than she expected."

Valerie leaned in. "She and I are going to help Rodney take the dresses that would have been in the fashion show and put them in a display."

Cleo opened her mouth to speak, then looked off to one side.

I followed her gaze to see Bryce Parker walking by on the sidewalk.

She turned back to face the group. For the briefest of moments, longing lingered in her eyes, but she blinked it away. "So, there won't be a fashion show?" she asked.

I shook my head, willing to play along as if I'd never noticed her staring at Bryce. "Not this year. Maybe in the future."

"That plan made a lot of sense to the board," Alice said.

"Even in just one day, though, attendance at the museum has already begun to pick back up." Imani had texted me the numbers at the end of the day. "So, I do think the museum will recover from its connection to another murder."

"I'm sure of it," Alice said. "People may have been nervous, but now they know the murderer is behind bars, thanks to you, Libby."

Warmth filled my chest. I was so lucky to have someone as supportive as Alice both as a friend and as the president of the museum board. "Not just me," I said. "Thanks to all of you."

"And I want to thank you as well." Valerie looked around the table. "I've had to face a lot over the past year. Losing our home and our community to the fire in California and then losing my husband. Being accused of murder on top of all that was almost more than I could handle."

Alice reached over and patted her shoulder.

Valerie pressed a hand against her chest, and her eyes shone. "But you worked together to clear my name, and you've renewed my faith in the people of Dogwood Springs. I'll be volunteering at the museum, I've found a faith community, and I've joined a local birding group. I think I can find friends here and build a real life."

"Of course you can," Alice said warmly, and everyone else murmured their encouragement.

I gazed at my dear friends, and gratitude welled up inside me. They had welcomed me to Dogwood Springs, and they had supported me—both in everyday matters and in times of life and death when we were solving mysteries. "Valerie," I said, "believe me when I tell you, you can make Dogwood Springs into a real home. It's a good place filled with good people. As you've seen, there are some exceptions, but most of the people really care about each other. And they'll care about you too."

I glanced at my dear, sweet dog, Bella, and then at the friends who had become as dear to me as family.

Zeke, who was getting ready to start his junior year at Dogwood Springs High School and who seemed so happy dating Zoe.

Alice, who was beginning her own educational adventure with her first real semester at Grove University.

Cleo, my best friend, who now not only ran her own business but also was purchasing property downtown and who—if my hunch was correct—might one day go out again with Bryce.

And Sam, wonderful Sam, who was starting a new business in addition to teaching at Grove University.

A smile spread across my face. Each of my friends, in one way or another, was starting a new chapter of their lives, and I would do my best to support them.

Epilogue

ONCE WE'D EATEN, Zeke pulled out his phone. "Sorry, guys, but I've got to go. I'm picking Zoe up after marching band practice."

Cleo stood. "And I need to run by my parents' house. Libby, are you still good with getting a ride home from Sam?"

I looked over at him, and he nodded. "Sure am," I said to Cleo.

Valerie and I both got big hugs from everyone, Bella got more petting and praise for being a heroine, and, eventually, we all left the café.

Cleo and Sam were both parked to the south, so the three of us walked out together with Bella.

After about half a block, Cleo's phone dinged with a text, then dinged again. She pulled it from her back pocket, stared at it, and stopped walking. She almost looked like she'd stopped breathing.

"Is everything okay? Did something go wrong with the sale of the salon?" I asked.

She drew in a deep inhale, her eyes grew wide, and a smile slowly spread over her entire face. "No, nothing's wrong." Her voice was quiet and a little shaky.

I exchanged glances with Sam.

Cleo held up her phone and turned it around so I could read the texts.

Bryce Parker
I drove out this evening and talked to Darcy's parents. After all the time she and I were engaged, I didn't want them to be blindsided. They were very understanding.

Would you like to go to dinner with me Saturday night?

I let out a squeal and pulled Cleo into a hug. "Oh, I'm so happy for you!" After a second, I stepped back and looked at her.

Her eyes shone. "Thanks. Hey, my car is this way." She pointed down a side street. "I'll talk to you later, okay?"

"Later," I agreed.

She headed down the side street, texting as she walked.

Sam stepped closer, grinned down at me, and then slid an arm around my waist. We continued on down Main Street, side by side, discussing Cleo's news. After another block, we came to Sam's car.

"Your blanket is ready in the back seat, Bella." Sam opened the rear passenger-side door for her.

She hopped in, and I was struck anew by how thoughtful Sam was. He didn't normally drive around with a stadium blanket in the back seat of his car. But as soon as I'd texted him to ask for a ride home from the café, he'd agreed, and he must have immediately gotten out Bella's blanket.

If it was anyone else, I might think they were worried about the damage Bella's toenails could do to the upholstery of the car and the expense involved in getting it repaired. But if Sam wanted to, he could buy a dozen cars. That blanket was there to make me more comfortable because he knew if something did happen to the upholstery, I'd feel terrible.

What a thoughtful guy. I could only hope Bryce would treat Cleo as well.

Sam held the front passenger door open for me, and I climbed in.

The sun hovered on the western horizon, filling the sky with glowing swaths of pink and orange and purple. To the east, clouds softly reflected the sunset's colors, surrounding us with so much beauty that we drove home mostly in a comfortable silence, only occasionally commenting when we turned a corner and saw another lovely view.

Soon Sam parked on Elm Street, and we walked to my front door. The heat of the day had dissipated, and the peeps of tree frogs were the only sounds on the street. With the excitement of catching Gene finally passed, and my delight over Cleo's news filling my heart, a deep sense of peace settled over me.

Peace and a niggle of curiosity. "Any word from the antique dealer?"

"Not yet," Sam said. "I'm dying to hear from her. After all the fun we had finding out about that painting, I'm totally on board with investigating another historical mystery."

"Me too." I stopped at my door and turned to face him. "But you do realize that letter may be a dead end, right?"

"With your ability to hunt down clues?" Sam chuckled. "I seriously doubt it. Which is why I'm so excited to see what that antique dealer says."

A tingle of warmth ran through my chest. I did know a thing or two about investigating historical puzzles that the average person didn't. And the possibility of figuring out a historical mystery with Sam was certainly something to look forward to.

"Mostly, though, I'm grateful you didn't get hurt, Libby." He took my hands in his. "When I thought about what could have happened if Bella hadn't been there, if you hadn't known how to defend yourself with that antique parasol ..." He blew out a heavy breath.

"I'm sorry. I didn't mean to—"

He pulled me closer. "Don't apologize. I love you the way you are. You're smart and brave, and you fight for justice. But if you ever try to trap another murderer, I want us to make better plans."

"I'm definitely in favor of that." I gazed up at him. How did I ever get so lucky as to have this wonderful man in my life?

Suddenly, Bella let out a bark and tried to wriggle between us.

"Just a minute, girl," Sam said to her. "I need to kiss your favorite human goodnight."

Bella sat down beside Sam, tail flopping against the porch.

"I want you around for a long, long time, Libby." Sam gently tipped up my chin. "You know how you worried that my parents might not like you?"

"Yeah."

"My dad told me he thinks you're the best person I've ever dated. My mom agreed."

"Really?"

"Really." He kissed me softly. "And I think they're right."

My stomach went all fluttery, and his words echoed in my mind. *Best person he ever dated.* Without a doubt, I could say the same about him. I stepped closer and threaded my fingers into his hair.

And he lowered his lips to mine.

My heart swelled. I had dear friends. I had the best dog in the whole world. And I had Sam, a man I trusted, a man who cared for me, a man who was as intrigued as I was at the possibility of solving another historical mystery.

What more could a woman want?

Thank you for reading this book!

Are you ready to return to Dogwood Springs for

another cozy mystery? Join Libby, Bella, and their friends in *Apples, Alumni & Animosity.*

A reunion ripe with secrets, and a killer among them.

When historian Libby Ballard is asked to offer a series of talks to a group of visiting university alumni, she's intrigued. When the offer comes with the promise of a large donation to the small-town history museum where she's the director, it sounds even sweeter. And when she learns the alumni are staying at a retreat center at a lovely local orchard, she readily agrees. What could be better than discussing her favorite topic in an idyllic venue filled with ripe red apples, happy friends, and hayrides?

Yet, the picturesque Missouri setting hides a poisonous secret. When one of the alumni is murdered, it becomes clear there's a bad apple in the bunch. With the sheriff baffled, and danger lurking among the leaves, the orchard's desperate owner asks Libby and her beloved golden retriever, Bella, to root out the killer.

As Libby investigates, she discovers that the alumni's relationships are rotted by long-held grudges and recent rage. If she wants to keep the reunion from culminating in another tragic goodbye, she'll have to act fast.

Curl up with Libby, Bella, and their friends as they delve into the core of this twisty mystery!

If you like a cozy mystery with a pet who will win your heart, friends who feel like family, and a hint of romance, you'll love *Apples, Alumni & Animosity.*

Don't miss your free reader bonuses! Join Sally's cozy mystery newsletter to:

- download the free five-chapter prequel to the Dogwood Springs series, BED & BREAKFAST & BURGLARY
- read exclusive content for every book, including a bonus chapter about Cleo's date with Bryce
- learn about new releases, and more!

Visit Sally's website at www.sallybayless.com/free-mystery/ to join.

See all the books in the Dogwood Springs Cozy Mystery Series at www.sallybayless.com.

Acknowledgments

With every book I publish, I realize more and more how lucky I am to have a supportive community to help me in the process.

As always, I owe a big thanks to the author friends who encourage me and to my editors, but with this book I want to say four special thanks.

To my readers: None of this would be possible without your support, dear reader! Each time you read one of my books, write a positive review, tell your friends to try one of my stories, or send an email or comment in my Facebook reader group to let me know you liked a book, you help make the next book possible! I can't tell you how grateful I am that you enjoy my writing.

To my beta team: After I finish writing each book, my beta team is invaluable. They give early feedback, asking questions and pointing out areas where I can make the story stronger. Thank you to Betsy Anderson, Laurel Bayless, Debbie Edwards, Barbara Hackel, Janice Huwe, Martha Burton Long, Kim Lyons, Carrie Saunders, and Stephanie Smith for beta reading this book. You made it much, much better!

To my cover designer: Donna Lynn Rogers of DLR

Cover Design is so talented and so wonderful to work with. I am incredibly grateful that you create my lovely covers!

To my family: Thank you to my husband, who is the first reader for all of my books. To my daughter, Laurel, who is a fantastic beta reader. And to my son, Michael, who is there to answer any tech questions. Thank you for all of your help and for cheering me on!

About the Author

After many years away, Sally Bayless lives in her hometown in the Missouri Ozarks. She's married and has two grown children. When not working on her next book, she enjoys reading, BBC mysteries, word puzzles, swimming, and shopping for cute shoes.